W9-CIN-299

Drawers & Booths

ARA 13

CovingtonMoore Publishing House
Texas

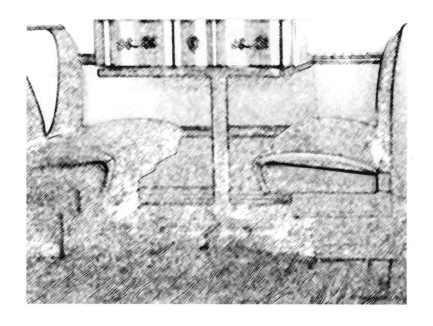

First edition copyright 2007 by Ara 13

All rights reserved. No part of this publication may be reproduced, stored in a retrieval system or transmitted in any form or by any means, electronic, mechanical, photocopying, recording or otherwise, without the prior written permission of the publisher.

Published in the United States by CovingtonMoore, Inc., in 2007. CovingtonMoore Publishing House, Texas.

ISBN 13: 978-0-9798636-0-8

Cover design by CovingtonMoore, Inc.

Printed in the United States of America.

Acknowledgments
Of Writing

A military journalist is used to having his work picked apart. My writing education truly began with the United States Marine Corps. In particular, my craft was honed by Chief Warrant Officer-4 (at the time) Tim Bennet. What luck to have his editing skills. Thank you to all eyes at every stage: Wayne Reed, Dana Sjostrom, Tim Thompson, and Michael Smith. Thanks ultimately to John Gorman for a diligent edit. Remaining errors are mine in the few instances I chose my wording over John's. Thanks John for your koreckshuns—u did a phine edut.

Acknowledgments
Of Friends

It has been my pleasure to befriend so many, though I have given back so little. Here is a minor reciprocation. Thank you Jessica Heidt and Jeri Johnson, Bill Hill, my idol Chuck Bachelor, Dan Rapka, (I remember) Jellineck and friends at SLU, Matt Gomes, George Ondish, Jen, Sean, Lenny and all the Tiners, partner in crime Trevor Snider, Kent Laborde, Peter Dean, Shawn Atkinson, Arledge, Troy Ruby, Tim Holden, few more influential than Torrey Hyatt, Stephanie Bok, Richard Hanft, always optimistic Mike Leta, Tim and all the Zellars to include Emma, Todd, Eric and Barb and all the Chases, Angela Brown and the crew at MOD, Carrie gives a shout out to Michael, Vic and friends at Quizno's, especially Corey for the faithful readership of my column, Trey Click, Laura McCalla, Shannon Keenon, Brynn, Dana, Jaimie, Misti, Steven, Robert, Stefan, Eddie, Amber, Fred and Tiffany, Jeff and Lauren, Andy, Paula, Matt and crew at Sky Bar, friends at Slices, my close friends and confidants Nina

Acknowledgments

Faulk and James Woolsey, a cut from the same block of wood as thyself Dan Woolsey. I exercised my artistic license in the spelling of your names. Fuck it, Thank You Dad, Brooks Hirsch, some of the genes were useful. Thank you Charlie Zellars, Jr. I can never repay your unswerving friendship. Perhaps, if I called occasionally, eh? I am sure I forgot people, and each omission will pain me. I ask your forgiveness.

Gail Ellen Hirsch, here is one big f-ing hug. All things I do are made possible only through you. May I be the same cornerstone in someone else's accomplishments. I would be just fine with that.

Thanks to all those who read this book. Love it or hate it or any level in between, thank you for your readership. I am one of you; it's just that I have your pocket change now. But, don't fret; I will likely blow it on books.

And finally, thanks to all the writers. It is my endeavor to be your peer. I especially thank Richard Dawkins, Sam Harris, Christopher Hitchens, and Michael Shermer for the education. How did I do?

Email comments to CovingtonMoore.com.

Drawers & Booths

LXXIII

PART ONE

Chapter One

The stench of burnt rubber mingled with the queer smell of cooked flesh. Barefoot villagers had beaten the man into submission with knobby tree limbs still bearing those green sprigs too pliable to remove without a machete. Women and young children braved approaching the prostrate petty thief and struck him with their bare fists. The man lay dazed—unable, even, to be demoralized by the frailty of his attackers. Several stronger teen-aged boys—more precisely, this country's men—penetrated the horde, dragged the wretched figure away, and propped him into a sitting position by ringing his torso with worn tires. They doused the entire concoction with petroleum and lit it. The man summoned enough energy to display agony. Soot escaped from the tires and into the air, reminding the Marine of an industrial smokestack. Even when the tortured screams ceased, the sound remained, resonating in the Corporal's head. The spectacle concluded with a large pop, and the Corporal broke from his transfixion, becoming self-aware, once again.

Two American soldiers stood from their jeep seats; a third dismounted and carried his M16-A2 rifle at rest—barrel aimed down and stock firmly against his shoulder so he could come to the ready and engage a target if necessary. It did not become necessary. If the soldiers had arrived sooner, this event would not have occurred. The people would not have doled out justice in front of a foreign audience.

The crowd of Cortinians dispersed, indignant yet ashamed in the American presence, leaving the charred remains to lie smoldering in the street. The flames futilely fought for life, as the rubber could not generate enough heat to sustain a fire. Smoke emanated from the seared face, as if the man were breathing hard in winter—not winter here, but back in the States. The Corporal knew no one would bury the body. He wasn't thinking of respect for the deceased, but of preventing disease caused by a festering carcass.

"What'll we do?" he asked the soldiers.

"Not my country; not my laws," said the driver.

"We should bury him," he half-heartedly proposed.

The vehicle guard smirked and remounted, and the driver put the jeep into gear.

"You OK here?" the driver asked.

The Corporal nodded.

"Did you get some good pictures?"

The Corporal looked down at his idle camera, having forgotten it had accompanied him. The soldiers drove off, kicking up a minor dust storm under the violence of the speeding tires. Even the earth opposed the military presence here.

Chapter Two

The Corporal's eyes began to tear, though not from emotion. The shock of the event had subsided, but the stench finally penetrated his senses. He returned his gaze to the body, overwhelmed by the vicious smell, yet his feelings, either non-existent or numb from overload, lay unmolested. He raised his camera and took a picture.

"What the hell am I gonna do with that?" Even if he pursued the villagers, they wouldn't talk. And even if they talked, the Corporal would never be allowed to submit the story. The military had a tenuous relationship with the host nation. A headline like: "U.S. Supports Savages" wouldn't go over well with the command. It probably would land him in the brig.

An elderly man peered back down the dry dirt road. The Corporal caught his eyes, raised the camera, and focused on the man as if to admonish him with a picture. The man cast his arms out shielding his face, turned, and hastened away. Many of the elders didn't want their pictures taken, distrusting any technology. Back in the States, people joked about third-world places where the uncultured believe pictures steal their soul. But here, the belief was literal, and the humor absented in the pain of this land.

He laid his camera-laden arm back against his side opposite the Beretta 9mm on his right hip. The Corporal inculcated carrying his camera in his left hand so he could draw his revolver with his dominant hand. He took the sidearm to Cortinia instead of the M16 to be more mobile, hands free to take pictures, providing the events before him didn't stun him into a comatose trance. Also, because most of the enlisted personnel didn't have an option to carry a pistol, the 9mm made the Corporal feel unique—a simple vanity.

The Marine would make his way back to the box and report the body to the engineers. They would likely cover it with lime or take it to a location away from any water supply. The villagers seemed to care little about their own health. And the soldiers—who didn't care at all— were the only ones taking action to safeguard civilians from disease.

The Corporal hoofed it back to the box and approached the gate guard.

"You're a Marine?" the guard asked from behind the thin latticed fence of 432's initial barricade.

The Corporal affirmed even though his branch was self-evident—his sleeves were rolled inside out in the fashion of the Navy and Marines, and the name tape said "U.S. Marines" plain as day.

"What are the Marines doing here?"

"I'm operationally accommodated by the Army Hospital. I'm PAO."

"You're a reporter?"

"Yeh."

"You can't bring that camera in here," the guard motioned with his rifle.

"Yes, I can. It's part of my issue."

"There's no photographic equipment allowed in the box."

"I *am* in the military, you know. I don't take any pictures inside. If I did, I'd get written up, lose a stripe, or go to the brig. I know my job."

"I'll have to call," said the guard and ducked into the shack.

The Corporal grew angry. He hated the insinuation he would run amok breaching operational security, as if he were a common civilian reporter taking advantage of the military's hospitality.

The gate guard returned. "You can't come in."

"Who'd you call?"

"The TOC."

"Did you tell them who I was?"

"They don't know you."

"They know me. I talk with Colonel Habersham every couple days."

"Who's that?"

"The unit commander."

"Not my unit," said the guard.

"Which TOC did you call?"

"432's."

"That's not the one I work with."

"It's the one I take my orders from, and they say they don't know you."

"Call the other head-shed."

"Can't—the phone is a direct line to our TOC. Besides, I don't have to. You're not coming in."

"You're gonna piss off a bird," said the Corporal.

"Not my bird."

The box was *all fouled up* with two commands, neither communicating with the other. One command delegated the notional entrance list. The other, controlling security, physically ran the gate. Between the two, no one came in or out. It was best to personally know a guard and get around the commands altogether.

"You need to clear the area," the guard flexed.

The Corporal stood agape. He wanted to go into a tirade. "Or what?"

"Or I'll have you arrested."

The threat was limp in its matter-of-factness. The Corporal could get arrested just to raise a stink, but this was not the battle to pick. "OK," he acquiesced then remembered why he had come. "I just wanted to report a body, anyway."

"U.S.?" the guard perked up.

"No, host-nation."

"Oh," he replied, deflated. "You still can't come in."

7

The Corporal nodded. "Should I tell you where?" he asked referring to the corpse.

"Go ahead," said the guard, disinterested.

"Are you gonna report it?"

"Probably not."

The Corporal snorted, turned and walked away. The body would rot in the streets. No one would care. The Corporal really didn't care either. He was more concerned about the six-mile trek to the Army hospital than any unknown body in an unknown street of an unknown place.

The MASH unit lay only two miles from the box, but the engineers were still sweeping the back road for mines laid from past civil conflicts, so the only open route was along the perimeter. Once the command opened the connector, the Corporal still had to gain entrance to the box to cut through to the hospital. He had to clear up his access problems. Perhaps, he could do a story on the gate guards to loosen them up. Everyone loved to see their name in the papers—except Intelligence. Right now, security saw him only as a threat. He would just have to keep his ears open for the appropriate time to impress the appropriate people.

Chapter Three

The absence of peddlers was not a good sign. When the Corporal first arrived, solicitors would accost him wherever he went, attempting to sell him candy, most likely given to them from soldiers' MREs. Sometimes, they would peddle minor military supplies either stolen or traded for who knows what service they provided. Even though the Corporal had no intention of buying anything, he enjoyed looking through the villagers' goods just to hear the idle gossip. Peddlers talked incessantly—a trait of salesmen regardless of country. Most of the U.S. soldiers remained in the compounds, and those who met up with the peddlers were usually part of a security force, hypersensitive to the potential for a terrorist bombing, and stayed clear of the goods or motioned the peddlers away from behind their M16s. Tell a soldier he's here to help people like the peddlers, and he would look at you uncomprehendingly. The host nation was only a tactical consideration—a notion—stunning the soldiers every time citizens materialized. In short, *they were a pain in the ass*. The country would be so much easier to help if it were devoid of civilians. And if the civilians were removed, most soldiers wouldn't see the irrelevance of the United States' military presence.

The Corporal wished a peddler would accost him now. The road was eerily quiet. The villagers, like birds in the brush, took off when something big was afoot—often the arrival of a predator. *Where were the peddlers? What did they sense … know?*

The Corporal broke leather and palmed the grip of his 9mm. He'd rather have the M16 now. He concentrated on seeing the first red-and-white striped, cement, road barrier, as if he could make it appear by yearning. As he approached the block divider, he grew more anxious, afraid to let down his guard so near to safety, as if bad karma were waiting for his ease of mind. He told himself being shot so close to security was a dramatic creation for movies—B-thrillers in which a woman being stalked is attacked at the moment she feels relief, keys in hand at her home door.

He sidled around the first barrier and crossed the lane toward the gap at the end of the second concrete divider. The barriers were positioned so vehicles must snake around, preventing anyone from approaching the gate with great speed. After the third barrier, he made a beeline for the gate and unhitched the latch himself while the gate guards eyed him from inside their concrete-and-sandbag-encased enclosure.

"You allow anyone to let himself in?" chided the Corporal.

"We seen you."

"What … no welcome mat? You don't miss me anymore?" The Corporal noted the guards remained inside their shed.

"Nah, uh," the first guard replied through freshly applied face paint. "Snipers," he added, nodding toward the woods.

"Bullshit. You're just bored."

"Nah, uh, Op4's in town."

"I've been in town. The only things there are some tires and a village thief, all of which have been recalled."

"You didn't see nothing else?" asked the guard.

"No, why? What's up?"

"82nd Airborne. That's what's up."

"Who told you that?" inquired the Corporal, incredulous.

"I don't know," the guard said and resumed his watch down the dirt road.

The Corporal grinned, snapped his holster closed, and opened the second gate. "You guys need anything?" he offered, closing the gate behind him.

"No thanks, Marine."

Inside the compound, the perimeter guards were doubled. Perhaps he passed security forces hidden in the woods—part of a heightened alert. *Why wasn't he informed?* He hadn't seen his captain for two days. *'Keep your troops informed.' Ever hear of that, captain?*

He crossed the compound and passed motor-transport's high arching tent, big enough to drive a truck through, yet now housing only various tools and vehicle parts strewn out on torn cardboard pieces to keep the greased objects off the dirt. A soldier lay on a crate, head and legs protruding beyond the ends, face up and shaded with his cover. Though precariously maintaining his awkward sleeping position, he was too lazy to find or create better comfort.

The Corporal unzipped his tent door, and the onrush of cold air stopped him at the entrance. The open flap let enough light into the dark tunnel for him to make out the straight route he would have to travel blindly once he let the flap close. A soldier mumbled something from under his poncho liner and rolled away from the intruding brightness. These were the night guards. The Corporal shared a tent with the enlisted security guards since he was the sole enlisted public affairsman, and the guards usually had a spare cot because the soldiers in this tent were continuously shuffled between duties. In some ways, they too were odd-men-out since they weren't real security forces but medical assistants relegated to guard duty because they were low men on the medical-team totem pole. *If this operation was other than a humanitarian mission, there would be real security forces, not nurses with night vision goggles, right?*

He closed the flap and edged his way blindly toward his cot, careful not to step on any of the warped planks and rock a sleeping soldier awake.

"Is that you, Marine?"

A "sshh" barely rose above the noise of the generator.

"Yeh."

"See any gooks?"

"Shut up, asshole!" said another soldier. "There aren't any gooks. This isn't Vietnam."

"Gooks, spics, whatever."

"Shut the fuck up! I'm trying to sleep!"

"I didn't see any," said the Corporal.

"No one? It's supposed to be a fucking war out there."

"Gordy, if I gotta fucking come down there …" came another warning from the recesses of the dark.

"Who said there's combat?" The Corporal's eyes began adjusting to the darkness, and he could make out Gordy sitting up in his sleeping bag.

"That's the word," Gordy replied.

"Last warning!"

"Shut up, I'm trying to sleep!" mocked Gordy. The Corporal heard stomping across several planks and saw a large, semidressed figure eclipse Gordy. A chest and fist thudded together, and Gordy exclaimed, "Ow, fuck. All right," then the plodding sound across the planks again into the dark recess near the generator.

The Corporal dropped his camera onto the cot and considered taking off his bucket helmet like the other soldiers, but he didn't feel right about going uncovered, especially since others expected him, a Marine, to adhere to customs. Besides, the Kevlar helmet reminded everyone he had access out of the box.

He continued down the tent toward the AC ventilation tube and quickly through the flap. Sergeant Porter stood behind the generator, swishing whiskers and shaving cream from his razor's head by dipping it into the water of a canteen cup resting atop the vents of the generator. He raised the blade toward his neck and shaved by feel, guided by his free hand.

"When'd ya get back?" asked Porter.

"Just now."

"The gate's closed. No one in or out."

"They let *me* in," said the Corporal.

"You're different."

"There was a patrol unit out too."

"Not from here," assured Porter.

"What's going on?"

The sergeant wiped his face dry with his green hand towel. "When you find out, let me know." He dumped his cup onto the dirt, the pool of watery shaving cream and whiskers bubbled atop the sere ground. Porter flipped open the flap of the tent and let the light pour in. "Wakey, wakey … eggs and bakey!" he bellowed and was received by the groans of the soldiers on second-shift.

Chapter Four

The Corporal passed several tents with their side flaps tied up. He avoided eying the soldiers sitting on their cots, playing cards, eating MREs, or just staring at passersby. Walking as if he had a purpose—quickly and eyes forward—he came to the tactical operations center, unzipped the flap, stepped in, and zipped the flap closed behind him.

"Marine on deck!" yelled the guard seated behind a metal desk, mockingly popping to attention. Several officers looked over at the Corporal; some smiled, some merely returned their focus on what previously held it. The S-2 officer didn't look up from his papers. The Corporal wished he had some information for the intelligence officer just so he could be acknowledged, as if only S-2 could validate his military worth.

"Hey, Marine," called Lieutenant Franklin—a huge black man, looking more at home in the Florida State University defensive line than behind an operations officer's desk. The Corporal returned the generous smile and stood somewhat at attention, knowing the formality was eschewed anyway.

"Sit, relax." The lieutenant gestured toward a chair. "How's the front?"

"Saw more stuff I can't write about."

"Like what?"

"The villagers burnt a man for stealing." S-2 looked up. The Corporal waited for him to ask about it, but he didn't.

"Why are you here if you can't write about that stuff?" asked Franklin.

"I'm here because the captain's here."

"And he's here as an interpreter, not PAO. That still doesn't explain why *you're* here."

"He can't write those glorious stories about himself, can he?" the Corporal half-joked.

The lieutenant smiled wide. "So you're just here for the ride."

"I begged him to take me."

"Why on Earth?"

"It's better than writing about officers' wives' luncheons … no offense, sir."

"None taken. Have you eaten?"

"No, sir."

"Come, we'll hit chow." He stood. "Don't you want to take off your brain bucket?"

"I'm under arms," reminded the Corporal.

"You're what?"

"I'm wearing my sidearm."

"Like anyone here is gonna know what Marines are supposed to do. Take it off; I'll take the blame." The Corporal gladly removed the Kevlar helmet.

"Why is the gate closed?" the Corporal asked, nonchalantly.

"What do you mean?"

"No one's allowed in or out."

"The gate's not closed," interjected S-2. "You got in; didn't you?"

The Corporal wanted to contradict the lieutenant, but he didn't want to rat on the guards. S-2 stared through the Corporal, thinking. "Thompson!" he yelled.

A sergeant bounded over to the S-2 desk. "Yes, lieutenant?"

"Go get Second Lieutenant Hall, A-SAP."

"Yes, sir."

Franklin and the Corporal followed the sergeant out of the TOC, and the lieutenant zipped the flap closed.

"Shit, sir; I think I just dropped a dime."

"Well, they can't be closing the gate if they're not ordered to. How would we get to the civilians?"

"Security doesn't believe in civilians."

The lieutenant laughed and stopped in the alley between the corner of the supply tent and the back of the TOC. The ground was riddled with stakes and ropes so one had to tread as if walking along a raised hopscotch board. Franklin turned and became serious. "Listen, I know your captain has been away quite a bit. Do you need anything?"

"No, sir. I'm good. Sergeant Porter has been taking good care of me."

"You got a cot?"

"Yes, sir. Thank you, sir."

"OK. You know that if you need anything …"

"Yes, sir. Thanks."

The lieutenant continued on toward the mess tent. "You guys got air conditioning now too, huh? It's a regular Club Med in there. Guys and girls … air … what's next, a hot tub? I suppose you've never seen it so good. They didn't treat you like this down the road, did they?"

"No, sir."

"No air in your tent?"

"No tent around my air," said the Corporal.

"They didn't make you sleep outside?"

"I kinda liked it, except for that night with the fire ants."

"How's your hand?"

"Good, since they lanced it."

"Let me see." The Corporal had wondered if the lieutenant had a medical background. If he had, Franklin would unflinchingly grab his hand and examine it like an object as did the other nurses. Instead, the lieutenant waited for the Corporal to display his hand and made a disapproving, nonclinical "yuk" expression.

"It's still swollen. Have you put anything on it?" asked Franklin.

"Yeh."

"Yeah, right." Franklin grabbed his tray and proceeded down the food line. "They didn't have the captain sleep outside too, did they?"

"No, sir. He stayed in some officer's quarters."

"What were you guys doing over there?"

"He did his thing with the CI teams, and I helped set up tents."

"Tents you couldn't sleep in," jested Franklin.

"Yes, sir."

"And now you're in Club Med," the lieutenant concluded. The Corporal noted Franklin's use of a tie-back ending and smirked.

They used a hospital tent's generator as a table and stood eating their spaghetti and meatballs, salad, corn, and brownie-like dessert—their dinner, the night guards' breakfast—and washed it down with *bug juice*. The Corporal often ate in silence, but Franklin didn't let food intake kill his conversation.

"What's this about the gate being closed?"

"My misunderstanding, sir."

"Look, I'm not about to turn you into an informant. The gate is not my jurisdiction," said Franklin.

The Corporal chortled. "They seem to think there are Op4 out there, and the 82nd is being sent in."

"The 82nd is not coming." Franklin grinned at his forkful of spaghetti. "You haven't seen anything, have you?"

"No, sir. But, I'm seeing fewer peddlers on the road. Actually, no peddlers on the road."

"What's that mean?"

"I don't know, but it made me nervous."

Franklin shook his head. "This is a humanitarian mission. There are no Op4. Damn gate guards think they're Marines. They want any excuse to paint up."

They finished their meals and returned to the TOC. On the way, the Corporal got a few stares from new faces unsure of what to make of a sole Marine. In the tent, he sat with the lieutenant and listened to him shoot the breeze with the other officers just long enough to relax, but not long enough for them to wonder why he had all this idle time, though everyone did—most were just masters at looking busy. After a mindfully timed rest, the Corporal snapped on his helmet.

"Thompson, who's first tonight, guys or girls?" asked Franklin.

"Guys got first hour."

"Are you gonna get a shower tonight?" Franklin asked the Corporal.

"I rarely miss one. Thank you, sir." The Corporal performed his modified position of attention. Though not in a combat environment, no one saluted since the colonel didn't acknowledge it, and he set the pace for the rest of the unit. If the environment changed, if there really were opposing forces, the Corporal would also cease popping to attention. He had never been in a combat environment and was uncertain if standing at attention was just as inappropriate as saluting. It would seem so. He'd have to ask his captain.

The Corporal returned to his quarters where the day guards milled about the tent, conversing and doffing their gear while Lieutenant Hall admonished them for the same reasons she had gotten chewed out by the S-2 officer, except she had stood at attention during her berating. The guards didn't take her seriously enough to give her that respect, and she foolishly tolerated the subordination.

"At ease!" yelled Porter, quieting the guards.

"Thank you, sergeant. Now, I don't know how it started, but ..." she hesitated and looked at the Corporal.

"He's OK," said Porter.

"This is not for print," Hall told the Corporal.

"Do you want me to step out?" he asked.

"He's like one of us, Ma'am," said Porter.

She hesitated.

"I'll go hit the head," the Corporal decided for her, exiting the tent. He opened the door to a porta-potty, peered into the corners, under the seat, and even into the roll of toilet paper for spiders before occupying the john. When he first arrived here, four days passed before he had the urge to sit down and use the bathroom, as his body adjusted to the shock of losing comfortable facilities. After his head-call, the Corporal stopped at the water buffalo, rinsed his hands and filled his two canteens.

At his quarters, most of the guards had left the tent for chow. Specialist Bryant was sitting on the rack with Chavez, his private first class girl-friend—a buff little Puerto Rican-American, who could outrun, out-pull-up, and out-push-up most of her platoon—except for Bryant.

"Am I interrupting anything?" asked the Corporal. "Maybe you guys want me to leave too?"

"She didn't say anything important," said Chavez.

"You're gonna miss chow," he reminded the two soldiers.

"Yeah, we're going. We'll work out later, OK?" she said.

"What do you want to do?"

"Push-ups, dips, whatever," Chavez replied, shadow boxing in front of the Corporal as if challenging him to a fight.

"Com'on, Ali," said Bryant, directing her by her shoulders out the tent.

After chow and following the workout, the males went to the showers while the females guarded the weapons. Before the females had returned from the showers, the Corporal turned in, dressed for a cold night, enhanced by the air conditioner, left running so the night crew didn't have to wait two hours for the tent to cool during the heat of the day when it was their turn to sleep. It was easier for the night-sleepers to bundle up than for the day-sleepers to get comfortable sweating atop their sleeping bags. Besides, no one there was concerned about an electric bill. Huddled in his sleeping bag with his poncho liner, the Corporal tried to ignore the sound of isolated amorous moments, some between two people, some likely alone.

Chapter Five

"Corporal … Marine, wake up." Someone was shaking him. It was dark, and he was tired. *This didn't make sense.*

"Not now," he murmured.

"Corporal, it's me, Porter." *Porter wouldn't be joking around. Something was important.* The Corporal forced himself awake.

"What's up?"

"The colonel's asking for you."

The Corporal pulled his legs out of the sleeping bag and groped for his boots. "Did he say what it's about?"

"No. I was told to find either you or your captain."

"Thanks." The air bit at his face and arms, but he ignored it in his haste to pull on his gear. "Did you look for the captain?"

"I wouldn't know where to start."

"Thanks, sergeant." He felt important, having to be roused in the middle of the night to see the colonel, but he couldn't fathom for what.

The night air, though cold, felt a good deal warmer than inside the tent. The surrounding tents' flaps were down, contrary to daytime when they appeared like some strange red-light district—window-displays of soldiers playing poker and eating pogey bait while staring at passersby with tired indifference. The encampment sat ghostly quiet, yet well-lit by the large overhead lamps positioned just inside the perimeter. The Corporal thought of knocking on the outside flap of the TOC tent as if he were a late-night visitor to someone's home, but the idea seemed ludicrous. He unzipped the flap, stepped into the TOC, and closed the flap behind him. A specialist he did not recognize popped to attention from behind the front desk.

"At ease, soldier," said Franklin, approaching the desk. "He's just a Marine, relax." Franklin wore his brown shirt and BDU pants, which dangled over his boots like civilian garb. His hair lay dented on one side from his recently bedded head. "Sorry to wake you, Corporal, but I thought this was a matter for you."

"I was told the colonel wanted to see me."

"He just left, but we decided these people should meet you."

"Who?"

"There are two civil affairs officers in the colonel's—I guess you would say—office."

"What's civil affairs?"

"Hell if I know, but I thought it can't be too different from public affairs, right?"

The Corporal shrugged, uncertain. "What do you want me to do?"

"Talk to them, I guess. We just thought, 'civil affairs, public affairs …' I don't know what we thought. We just told them they should talk with you."

"Yes, sir."

From across the tent, a lieutenant on night-duty stared at this Corporal who was called to meet the two late-night visitors, fueling the Marine's feeling of importance. Franklin led the Corporal into the colonel's section.

"Major Johnson, Lieutenant Kick, our resident Marine."

The Corporal popped to attention, but acknowledged each officer by visually addressing him. "Major, … lieutenant."

Johnson offered his hand, and the Corporal came at ease for the gesture. "Sir," he said, shaking the major's hand. The lieutenant remained still, his evaluative mien a polar contrast to Johnson's gaping smile and casual manner.

"Relax," said the major.

"At ease," said Franklin. "Or, I guess you are at ease," he realized. "Just cut that out; chill, will you. You can do push-ups in the rain later. Damn jarheads."

The Corporal partially relaxed and smiled, "Yes, sir."

"Kick used to be a Marine, or still is … what is it, 'once a Marine, always a Marine'?"

"Yes, sir," said Kick coldly. He wore jump wings on his uniform, and both civil affairs soldiers wore airborne patches. The Corporal felt slightly phony.

"So, besides the colonel, you're the only connection with the civilian population?" asked Johnson.

"I'm not sure, sir."

"Well, from what I understand, other than direct medical care, there is no interaction with the population."

"I've seen some patrol units, but that's about it, sir." The Corporal was unsure of what the major meant by *interaction*. He hadn't seen any fighting, if that's what he was being asked, but he felt it prudent not to probe.

"You're just a reporter, right?" Kick nearly admonished, as if he were trying to establish the futility of talking to the Corporal.

"He's PAO," said Franklin.

"What's that mean?"

The Corporal explained, "I've also been trained in public affairs matters—dealing with the civilian media and community relations."

"See, L-T," said the major, "he does some of the same things we do, but back home. He just has no experience dealing with host-nation civilians." To the Corporal he inquired, "Do you know what we do?"

"No, sir."

"Our job is to win the hearts and minds of the people," said Kick, sounding rehearsed.

"We are the go-between for the civilian population and the military," said Johnson. "We deal with all aspects of civilian life, not just medical like here in the MASH unit. We deal with legal issues, matters of public utilities, relocation, and such."

"Why would they be relocated?" The question slipped out. The Corporal knew he would not get away with inquiries like this in a Marine unit. Yet, he was wary of appearing incompetently obsequious—even if he did risk Kick's rebuke.

The major chuckled, downplaying his slip. "That's an extreme example. Right now, we need to establish a C-MOC—sort of a civilian/military information tent—and we could use your assistance in interacting with the people since you have already established some ties."

"You would need to talk with his captain first," said Franklin.

"The Corporal's not with you?"

"No, sir. He is operationally accommodated by us, but he works for his captain—a Marine linguist assigned to a counter intelligence unit that came in with the other battalion."

"Why is a CI unit here for a humanitarian mission?" asked Kick.

"They are preparing for the president's parade. The captain is acting as an interpreter to help organize the event," answered Franklin.

"More likely, the captain came in with psy-ops," said Johnson confidentially to Franklin. "We'll talk. Thank you, corporal. Sorry to have roused you in the middle of the night."

The Corporal popped to attention, understanding he was being dismissed so the officers could talk. "Yes, sir. Thank you, sir, lieutenants." He turned and exited the TOC.

The warmth of the night air, in contrast to the air-conditioned tent, again surprised his bare face and exposed forearms. *What was all this talk about psy-ops—that's psychological operations, isn't it? Relocation of civilians?* He'd have to ask his captain.

"Halt, who goes there!"

"Moody, it's me."

"I said HALT!"

"Moody, if you don't get that fucking M16 out of my face, I'm gonna stick it up your ass."

"Damn it, Corporal, why didn't you identify yourself?" he said, lowering the rifle.

"What's your fucking problem? I'm in the middle of camp, and you're playing with live ammunition."

"I don't know who's walking around out here."

"Who the hell do you think's walking around out here, Saddam Hussein?" he derided and stalked away to his tent, angry and no longer thinking about the MASH unit's new residents and what he didn't know about his own captain.

Chapter Six

"Wake up, shitbags. It's show time!"

"Aww, fucking-a, already?"

"Get up, get up, get out of the rack!"

"All right, we're up."

"Hey, Marine, you getting up?"

"Leave him alone, he had a late night rendezvous."

"I'm up, Sergeant P." The Corporal swung his feet out of the bag and into his boots, poised portside of his cot.

"What went on last night? Did you have to shoot a few gooks?"

"Shut the fuck up, Gordy," said Porter.

"Hey, sergeant, what's the deal with Moody? He got all gung-ho on my ass last night," said the Corporal, intentionally *throwing Moody under the bus* so the guard's excessive zeal could be dealt with in-house before it came to the officer's attention.

"Hey, Moody! What the hell happened last night?"

"My bad, Sergeant P. I didn't expect to see the Corporal out past curfew," he replied, dropping his web gear onto his rack. Half the soldiers were shedding their clothes for bed, while the other half dressed. Neither group appeared too lively.

"What curfew?" asked the Corporal.

"What curfew?" repeated the sergeant. "There's no freakin' curfew."

"Sure there is," said Bryant. "Lieutenant Hall set it at 2400 hours."

"The fuck she did. Don't you think the shift-leader would know?" said Porter, only to reconsider his position. "I'm gonna get to the bottom of this," he muttered and walked out of the tent.

"Damn, Corporal, what the fuck were you doing up last night anyway?"

"Leave him alone dumb-ass; he's got secret gook-shit to do," said Gordy.

"I was coming from the TOC," replied the Corporal, revealing just enough to insinuate great importance. The soldiers eyed him as he donned his gear.

Gordy uncouthly continued his line of questioning. "So, what's the deal? Is there gonna be a war?"

"Shut up Gordy. He can't talk about it, right, Corporal?" said Bryant.

"I don't know." He could see Sergeant Porter yelling at Lieutenant Hall through the open flaps of the tent, housing the public address system. Hall cowered like a berated dog and exited, head lowered. The Corporal left his quarters before Hall entered from the opposite end. He didn't want to be asked again to step outside so she could talk with her troops alone. He remembered Porter saying when the Corporal first arrived, "she's about as useless as tits on a nun. But I guess that's why she's in charge of *us*," the sergeant admitted.

Yesterday's MRE suited him better than the line for morning chow. Motor-T buzzed with the morning vehicles. The gate was open and active, and the air held that slight chill it harbors just after the sun comes up, when you'd expect it to warm the earth instead of drop the temperature with the rising air.

The noticeably antsy gate guards, anxious to be relieved of duty, bade the Marine *good morning*.

"Morning, guys, Chavez."

"Are they comin' yet or what?" she asked.

"Yeh, they're getting ready."

"Who's your new buddies?" she half-joked, gesturing with her chin to the tent beyond the front gate. Johnson and Kick were draping camouflaged netting over the entrance of a small visitor's tent and raising it with poles, creating an awning over four folding chairs. Outside the CA's tent stood a large hand-painted sign: *Civilian Military Operations Center.*

"I guess you won't be the only cool one walking around outside the gate now," said Chavez.

"No shit."

"Corporal, come over here," beckoned Kick.

"Yes, sir."

"Good morning, Marine," warmly greeted the major. "We tried to get in touch with your captain last night, but to no avail. Do you have a lot on your slate for today?"

Johnson's respectful inquiry doubled as a jab toward other's attempts to feign busyness.

"No, sir. What can I help with?"

"Well, I need to get a line run from the TOC into here, but I imagine that is something Lieutenant Franklin can help me out with, right?"

"Yes, sir."

"But, I was hoping you could take the L-T into town and show him around a bit."

"I'm particularly interested in meeting a Doctor Silas Johanson. Do you know him?" The Corporal noticed Kick had interrupted the major.

"Yes, sir. He comes to the gate every couple of days and asks to speak to the commanding officer."

"And what happens?" asked Johnson.

"They turn him away like all civilians."

"The colonel doesn't meet with any civilians?"

"No, sir. Only local authorities."

"The police?"

"Yes, sir."

"What about local military?"

27

"What military?"

The Corporal evaluated the major's smile. Kick stood on the balls of his feet as if to pounce if he must.

"Why don't we take a walk into town," Kick redirected.

"The doctor's a good guy. He's just frustrated, as are most of the people around here," the Corporal offered as his own attempt to ease the awkwardness.

"I understand that," said the major. "We hope to help them."

"Let's go, Corporal," said Kick, seeing no reason for small talk or to expound upon things he already knew.

"Oh, if your captain shows up is there anything you want me to relay?" asked Johnson.

"No, sir. I'm good." Though not a Marine, Johnson knew it was odd for the Corporal's officer to have abandoned him.

Kick slung his rifle, and the two men stepped off. They strode down the dirt road, leaving no dust trail, for the morning dew kept the earth aground. Kick's whistling seemed a contrived calm, and his right hand firmly holding the grip of his rifle belied his ease. With one rotation, he could have the sling off his shoulder and the butt tucked against the crotch of his arm. The Corporal searched in vain for a subject to broach. Again, the desolate roads were unnerving.

"So, how long you been a Marine?" The Corporal thought Kick's question was designed to remind him he too was a Marine.

"Almost four years."

"Been a corporal long?"

"Just picked it up."

"I was a meritorious sergeant."

"No shit."

"Yeah."

Kick scanned the woods, taking note of every creature on the ground, in the trees, and air. In life and in literature, nature disinterested the Corporal. He never could get through *Walden* because of its long descriptions of greenery. Leaves, shrubs, trees, gardens, birds, whatever; it all bored him.

Along the road was merely the incidental environment one must walk by to get to the people. Someone like Kick would be interested in all that crap and want to talk about it. The citizens revered a certain bird's nest almost as an icon. The Corporal considered bringing it up, but he didn't want to involve himself in a conversation about nature. He remained quiet, ignored the scenery, and played in his head the introduction of Kick to Doctor Silas.

The Corporal quickened his pace to turn the trek into a legitimate Marine Corps hump, not quite double-time, yet without the ten-minute rest in the just-under-two-hour trip. A meritorious sergeant should have no trouble keeping pace, he thought. It was silly to feel challenged, but he couldn't keep from proving his mettle. He could hear the pounding of the gravel behind, as if a trotting horse were on his heels. He feigned checking the scenery to his hard left, focusing on the peripheral image, trying to glimpse whether the ex-sergeant was trotting, unable to keep up with the Corporal's long strides—as if breaking from a *walk* was a sign of inferiority. But the lieutenant was keeping pace fine, still scanning the scenery for animal life.

"It's a small town, just three buildings," The Corporal yelled into the air in front of him, as if his words were a handful of grass tossed into the sky and carried by the wind into the face of the lieutenant behind.

"What are the other buildings?"

"A church and a local policeman's home. Doctor Silas lives at the clinic. And his nurse ... well, I'm not quite sure where she lives, but not there."

"Is it Father Atkinson's church?"

"Yes. How did you know?"

"From the area assessment."

"The what?" He turned to see the lieutenant's face. The lieutenant quickened his pace to pull abreast of the Corporal.

"We assess the area—find out key players and such."

"Like S-2?"

"Kind of. Their lists: the white, gray, and black are for gate access and other security measures. Ours are for social influence—networking. We also evaluate the land, facilities, and culture. For instance, I know not to try and shake the hand of the doctor's female assistant."

Had he intentionally kept that courtesy from Kick so he would make the faux pas? "Yeh, but she's American. I don't think it would be a big deal, but we both avoid it so as not to upset the civilians."

"Well, you can't be shaking a woman's hand out in public, can you? It's just indecent."

Having the culture to mock gave the lieutenant a chance to warm up to the Corporal, as if he wanted a co-conspirator. It reminded the Corporal of people telling racial jokes, assuming others would relate.

"They have their reasons." The Corporal wasn't ready to be chummy with Kick just yet. He still distrusted the man's manner and didn't want to be his accomplice to any future abrasiveness.

"Well, there's nothing like experiencing the country first-hand."

"Did you know they burn petty thieves by ringing them with tires and lighting them on fire?"

"No, I didn't know that one." Kick could give his full attention when interested.

"Sometimes, along back roads, I'll find human remains, bodies with gashes—hatchet wounds. Once, there were three skulls, nothing else, two small ones and one adult, all with gaping gashes in them. I used to tell the local police, but they'd just thank me without wanting to be shown the location. Then again, it's not like they have a forensics lab here."

"Have you ever seen any bones with holes in them?" asked Kick.

"What? Like with bullets?"

Kick nodded.

"No, sir. Besides, the only ones with guns over here are us and the police. Half the time, the police don't even have guns in their holsters. They're nice enough guys. Sure, if you try and talk with them about some crime, they'll just shrug as if there's nothing they can do. But if you bring up farming or the weather, they'll light up and bullshit with you all day."

"Is that right?"

"Yeh. It's all that really seems to matter to these people. They could care less about the damn parade my captain is working on, or even who's in power, just as long as no one fucks with their oxen."

"That's good to know."

The Corporal fell back into silence, happy to leave it with the lieutenant acknowledging the worth of his own assessment.

Chapter Seven

Soon, the parade of trees flanking the Corporal and Kick broke rank, revealing a makeshift settlement. It's one thing to be told a town is comprised of merely three buildings. It was another to witness the stark austerity of that reality. Three half-painted buildings stood defiantly atop a clearing of earth and dying grass. Two of the structures were void of entranceway doors. Only the private home of the police officer was closed to the outside.

Idle country people stood in the shade of the doctor's building, either waiting to be seen or simply taking a respite from the heat of day. The Corporal knew the people here were in no hurry. Back in the States, Americans got indignant when told by the cable company the hookup man would come between the hours of twelve and two. Here, it was not uncommon for a villager to wait ten hours for a doctor's visit, only to be instructed to come back tomorrow—and they took it in good stride.

The Corporal and Kick passed the waiting villagers in their half-hearted queue and stepped over the wooden lip of the doorway into the doctor's quarters. The two men interrupted a physical, as no reception area buffered the doctor's examinations from intrusion. This was third-world patient care. No paperwork. The patient's history was retained in the physician's head, augmented by the self-treatment stories of the individuals. Silas was currently working on the head wound of a woman with a piece of glass stuck in her scalp, which, although treated with local ointments, was festering. Nearly three weeks after the accident, she decided to make the eight-mile trek to Silas' and have it looked at. The common practice of villagers simply putting up with an injury until it was critical irritated Silas. He often saw near fatal cases that began as easily treatable minor injuries.

The doctor looked up from his dabbing, above the rim of his glasses, took note of the two visitors, and returned his attention to his patient before speaking. He offered no preamble. Silas' feelings of futility when dealing with the military had drained him of the customary niceties.

"It's the inverse of the cliché about not seeing the trees composing the forest. The medical team here is so entrenched in large-scale vaccinations, water treatment issues, and the like, they have no inclination to remove a piece of glass from one poor woman's scalp."

"What about the NGOs?" asked Kick.

Silas looked up. "I *am* the NGO in this town."

"How would you feel about visiting hours staffed by our people, and not just the medical personnel, but JAG lawyers, environmentalists, and whatever else is on your plate?"

Suddenly, the Corporal wanted to be associated with the lieutenant.

"I would say, *it's about damn time.* You people seem to think you can take a farmer's land, kill his soil, and leave him to fend without his livelihood, all so he can vote."

"Well, that's not how it was supposed to work," said Kick. "I'm a civil affairs specialist. My job is to give you and others the voice they need to resolve these issues."

"I have the voice; like Antony, it's the ears I need."

"Well then, I'll get you the ears too."

"Hm," was all the doctor could muster. He wasn't used to being accommodated by someone in camouflage. Silas sent an evaluative glance over to the Corporal. He would conclude the Corporal had a greater role in fostering this burgeoning alliance, an assumption the Corporal wouldn't dissuade.

"Give me a moment to finish up here, and we can talk," said Silas.

The Corporal and Kick stepped back outside. No one acknowledged them. The Corporal knew this was normal village life ... now, tomorrow, and years from now. Here, there would be no march toward progress, only indifference in these sun-beaten impoverished people.

"Was that the priest?" asked Kick, gesturing with two fingers in the direction of the whitewashed church.

"I didn't see," said the Corporal.

"Wait here for the doc. I'll go introduce myself. Maybe we can kill two birds with one stone ... develop two contacts on our first day. Not bad, eh?"

"No, sir."

Kick approached the church and stepped over the entryway frame. It was dark to his immediate sides, and the sunlit sanctuary made it harder for Kick's eyes to adjust to the recesses of shadows in his periphery.

"Father Atkinson?" he called.

"No," I reply, emerging from the dark.

Kick turns to his right. "Who the hell are you?"

"Nobody." I measure him up, wondering how he will react.

"You don't belong here," he senses. "What the hell are you doing? You are going to fuck everything up."

"How do you know I'm not with the Red Cross?"

"Don't fuck with me. We are well into the story, and here you are speaking first-person and ... and present tense! The readers are gonna immediately realize something is wrong!"

"Well, they will now," I quip.

"Get the fuck out of here!"

"In due time."

"What do we do?" Kick panics.

"Relax, no one is reading this. Do you know how hard it is for a first-time author to get published? It's just as hard to find an agent as it is for the agent to find a publisher … harder in fact."

"We're not supposed to talk about the process … about him," Kick whimpers.

"You mean the author? His name is Ara."

"Don't!" Kick covers his ears to the offense.

I laugh to myself over his foolish cowardice and can't help but to continue flaunting my dissidence.

"Of course, I suppose there is always self-publication, but Ara may be too proud for that. Even if he continues with this novel, he's likely to edit me out anyway. Either way, I doubt this will see the light of day."

"What'll we do?" Kick repeats.

"Well, the cat's certainly out of the bag, isn't it?"

Kick stares at me, catatonic.

Doctor Silas' patient exits the house, donning a new head bandage. The Corporal watches in awkward silence. The woman looks up and catches the Corporal's pensive gaze, shrugs her shoulders, hesitates, decides better of speaking, and continues on her way.

"You certainly caught me be surprise," says Silas, wiping his brow with his handkerchief while easily maneuvering over the entranceway frame, an act of habituation. "I never thought …" He stops short, lowering the kerchief. "Where's the lieutenant?"

The Corporal, at a loss for words, shrugs.

Silas continues awkwardly, "But I thought … Are we in present tense? That's odd."

"You better get back there," I advise Kick. "You'll stop the whole story in its tracks."

Kick simply nods like a chastised little kid and walks back to Silas' place, his arms pinned to his sides as if the weight of his anxiety robs him of extraneous movement.

Once the lieutenant departs, I consider leaving you, the reader, with the author's original story, but we should give the characters time to regroup and Ara a chance to repair his fractured narrative. Come …

35

Chapter Eight

I exit the military story and revisit an older scene just to get back into the right frame of mind. I was once on the force. I remember the matted down grass as if his body coincidentally fell into an abandoned deer bed. I had the inclination to look for the stag. Foolish, I know. I just couldn't shake the idea I was missing something; that I was supposed to look for more.

The lines of lividity suggested he had been dumped here already dead. Likely, he died face-up after being bludgeoned. We supposed the perp killed him somewhere else entirely. There weren't sufficient blood splatters anywhere around the field that would have accompanied so brutal a bashing as his body had received.

My instincts said this was no professional hit. It was sloppy. Unplanned. Or it was interrupted? The body was too easily found. *Why dump it nearly out in the open?* Later, we learned the killer had moved the body at night, that the area seemed more concealed in the dark than it was in actuality.

We worked the scene and gathered the clues: tire tracks, carpet fibers likely from a car's trunk, and some kind of automotive goop. Unlike the

TV shows, most of our detecting was blatantly obvious. Though his wallet was gone, we IDed the man from his finger prints. He was in the system. After just one interview of a friend—*if you can call her that*—we easily made his criminal connections and the location of the probable crime scene. We sent an undercover agent into the garage and easily got a warrant after the officer saw the blood splatter, which the idiots had been too lazy to even attempt to clean off the walls. We hit the shop and located traces of blood, half-heartily cleaned with bleach. I wasn't surprised; most criminals are lazy. These wizards completely overlooked the wrench still covered with blood and flesh. From body to arrest, we sealed their fate in two days.

They were a small-time ring. The hot vehicle parts, cameras, and video equipment were enough to hold them while the lawyers got their *ducks in a row* doing whatever they do to make their case. But the lawyers needn't have sweated it. The idiots turned on each other in interrogation.

"Got 'em," said Hockney.

I just nodded. I still had the feeling I was missing the bigger picture.

It was the first time I voiced my suspicions to Hockney, but he didn't get the same scent. "You heard it, Hattie; it's cut and dried. They got in a disagreement that got out of hand. One smacks the other; then it escalates to a wrench and bammo … there's no turning back after the first couple whacks. You either finish him off or you gotta worry about retaliation for the rest of your life. These aren't made guys. Strictly amateur-hour. There wasn't an *up high* for the order to come down from."

Hockney paused. "That's just the way it is." He hammer-punched my shoulder. "We did good, pal. Right?"

"Yeah."

Now, I know better. Those idiots weren't alone. But … aw, screw it. I sound desperate, like I'm trying too hard to convince you. Read on if you want, but I ain't rehashing the last year of my life now for your sake. I did what I had to do by revisiting the scene. I got my mind straight. It's getting late, or early … you tell me. How the hell am I supposed to know when you are reading this? Either way, I'm tired of hearing myself talk.

Chapter Nine

I suppose it's not entirely your fault. After all, I've lived my kind of life and you've had yours. But if you aren't a babe in the woods, I'm less apt to forgive you. Most adults should have had their suspicions. For those of you who are younger or have been living in a cave all your life, I'll cut you some slack. I'm still not gonna give you the big ol' lowdown. Let's say we ease you into my way of thinking, shall we? Why don't we start simple?

My apartment. What should I tell you about my apartment? I don't live here. I sleep and shit here. That's about it. Three stories, and the only place to sit is on my bed. There's no food in my fridge, my oven has never been turned on—hell, I don't even know if the pilot light is still lit. That's a problem, isn't it? No TV. I have a radio, but I just listen to books on tape: social deviance, Steven Pinker's *How the Mind Works*, etc.

I know I am rambling, but I just need to think. It's your rotten luck you're privy to these thoughts. But I'm telling you, just as sure as rain, he's out there. He's behind it.

My major epiphany came the day I sat with dummy number one at the pen. Normally, people like me don't get a one-on-one with the criminal of their choice, even if they arrested him. There are procedures for who interviews who, and I don't have the right letters after my name to open the right doors. I'm not a psychiatrist, professor of criminology, or such. But, I still had connections who knew I was no dope. I did my homework. I'd studied more on the subject of behavior than most with various fancy degrees. It's not unrealistic to think I, a near layman, can probe his mind and locate a chink in the fabric of his thoughts.

Like I said, I always had my suspicions—ever since my late teens. By the time I interviewed this guy, I was beginning to get a picture in my head. No ... different than a picture—a concept. I could feel the language wanting to form, assembling like a primordial ooze of words. Lately, my thinking seems to have this sense of Darwinian fitness, with the more adaptable concepts surviving, as if my ideas were getting more complex, building on the material before. I often reflect on where ideas come from, and I believe they are some kind of phase-shift, like water boiling, their potential suddenly realized seemingly out of the blue. I have a word I've tried to keep remembering ever since I was around eight: *wallaby*—the shoe, not the animal. Often, the idea that I have a word to remember comes to me before I realize the specific word. I intentionally appreciate the moment of not knowing, trying to be fully aware of the *eureka-moment*. I try to feel where it comes from, how it manifests in my brain. Then, like a grand respiration of crisp clean air, it wafts over me—*wallaby*.

Anyway, my point is that's how I felt before interviewing this guy, like I was waiting for that phase shift. There was some idea trying to get out. I needed to think like I was trying to remember a song and block out everything else while humming that one fractured refrain, the only clue I had. That's why I went to the jail and met with the prisoner. I needed to hold the semblance of the *wallaby-like* aura intact, though I felt I only had it by a thread.

Again, this was nearly three years ago—just a few days after his confession. I was seated at the sturdy metal table when the guard brought him in. He didn't seem surprised to see me, perhaps because he didn't know this wasn't the norm. The magnitude of his circumstances still had him in mild shock. If he hadn't pled out the previous day, I never could have talked with him without his lawyer. For possibility of parole, he gave up his entire criminal ring of small-time hoods, all of whom had been doing fairly well robbing vendors at weddings and such events. They would dress up in nice suits, walk into the reception and haul off the professional camera and video equipment, either being mistaken as assistants or overlooked completely. He ratted out six of his fellow thieves. His agreement was written in nice legalese and signed by several lawyers. His case was nearly over. He had nothing to lose, and was looking for new friends—anywhere.

I forced my initial small talk. I even let him ramble on for a minute or two about the dog races, though I couldn't have given a crap. Finally, I segued to the night of the murder.

"Tell me how it started," I began.

"He just didn't want to listen," the big lug whined. When it came right down to it, he was just plain weak. Later, he would develop a harder crust, and I'd get no more out of him. I had to interview him when I did, before he could think about what he was saying, before the defensive filter was installed.

"But can you remember the moment before it got out of hand?" I probed.

He adjusted his weight in the metal chair. "I know what you're looking for: You want a light that switched on. There was never no light that just switched. I was always mad at him. I could have killed him over a dozen times before. I'm made that way." He continued matter-of-factly. "I'm no good-guy that suddenly went too far. I lived my life over the line."

"And it was just the two of you?"

"What are you looking for? Don't you think if there were a third person in the garage I would have dropped the dime by now to get less time?" he said unabashed at his crass disloyalty.

He turned his gaze to the upper corner of the room. "God knows if

my Nana was there, she'd have stopped me from going too far. But they
can't watch over you all the time, can they? I guess that's why you got
to beat sense into some kids, huh?"

That's when it hit me like a ton of bricks: *Wallaby.*

I suppose to you, the reader, this mook's declaration nixes a third
party. But I don't know how much you know, how wide your eyes are.
It's clear as day to me now. Perhaps, if you weren't caught up in this
book's previous pages—some modern-day, "what is our military's role,
now?"-bullshit, you'd be more receptive, and your eyes would be as wide
as mine. Sorry if I don't have much patience. It's daunting thinking
about getting you up to the speed.

You do have an option. Skip ahead. Go back to the war story if you
want. The Corporal, lieutenant, Silas, even that patient with the head
wound—they're all dead. Op4 came in and wiped them all out. Shot up
everyone.

Anticlimatic, isn't it? What's the matter; is that a little too realistic?
People dying without mood music. Did you invest too much emotional
energy to merely learn third-person they died before they had reached
their true potential? Welcome to the real world.

If you were wondering, Ara didn't kill them off, like some pseudo-
Hitchcock thriller, leaving the reader to wonder who the true lead
character is. No … don't look at me like that. It wasn't me. I don't have
that kind of ability. As you can tell from all my short, choppy thoughts,
I'm no writer. It was him, my quarry He's covering his tracks.

It may have been a good story; I don't know. I'm sure you recognized the buildup: The inquiry about bullet wounds, the confusion of
security by the gate guards, the rumors of Op4 and the 82nd Airborne.
Where else do you think the story is going? Ara is gonna end it with some
allegorical bullshit about men falling from the sky.

Is that you? Oh, shit. It's my cell phone. Hold on …

Ara 13

Displaced People

Sorry, that was Hockney. There's been another murder. I know, murder is the term used after the conviction, but I told you, I'm no writer. Let the editors haggle over what's what.

"This is the last time," Hockney says at the scene. "My allegiance can only go so far."

"I'm not going to give up," I tell him. "I know I'm right."

"You're making a fool out of us. Me … I gave up caring about how you look long ago. But I gotta protect my unit—my men; not to mention, her." He points to the little girl lying in the dirt with her panties around her knees. "I have to respect her memory. Her parents need closure, not some hypothetical, megalomaniacal overlord."

I don't understand him. He probably sounds sane to you, but you are just like him. I don't know why you guys don't see it.

"Hattie, some things are just what they are. There's no reason for this. There's no connection."

"That's exactly my point," I say.

"What?" He is losing his patience with me. "Some guy is randomly killing people in a variety of different ways just for shits and giggles— a guy who's so smart, he's able to set up all kinds of shitheads, who for some reason won't drop the dime?"

"Or they don't know." Hockney didn't expect me to agree and expound upon the assessment.

"For fuck's sake," he whispers, "I heard you were up in Peru at that mass casualty from the mudslide. The rumors are getting a life of their own."

"I *was* there," I confess.

Hockney becomes serious, authoritatively firm. "This is the last one. I'm not calling you after this."

"It's OK. I've seen this one before."

"I don't even know what the fuck that means!" He walks away with his arms up in surrender.

I *have* seen it before. Little girl raped and throttled. It's the consistency of these acts I find so fascinating. In a society like ours, you would expect reasonable people to do whatever they can to discourage—no—flat out *stop* this from happening. What would we do if we had unlimited resources? How would we prevent this and all our other ills?

Her face would be cherubic were it not absent the hale rouge. Her parents lost sight of her as they stopped at a convenience store on their way to a dance recital or school play, or some such nonsense that had caused them to put her in an adult-looking dress with a ribbon in her hair and makeup—not that I am blaming her attire. It's just the fact of the matter—the touches that probably sparked the rapist's attention. But, it's not him I am looking for. It is the other one. The one who wasn't there ... or was and watched. Sick, huh?

Let's go.

Chapter Ten

I used to collect clippings. Now, there's no sense. I amassed so many news articles the collecting became an obsession in itself. I don't want to become one of those people who spend more energy making to-do lists than doing the tasks. Hell, now I'm rambling again. Are you even listening?

What … again? Wait. There's no reason for you to go anywhere. I'll answer it here.

"Hello?"

"This is Detective Brocco from New York City. I'm looking for Hattie Shore. I'm not sure if I got the right number."

"You do; that's me."

"Do you know a Roger Pearson?"

"The name doesn't ring a bell."

He grunts. "Well, someone here seems to know you."

"Has there been a homicide?" I ask, taking a stab.

"Are you a cop?" he replies, delaying answering my question.

"I was once." Why explain further and spook him right off the bat by seeming like a conspiracy nut?

"Well, I don't know what you would call it. But you are being addressed by someone. I've been kind of hoping you could tell us more."

"I'll fly into Newark and rent a car. I'll call you back in about twenty minutes from a land line. I'm in my car now, and I can't write down directions. How long do you think it will take me to get there from Newark?"

"Half an hour or so depending on traffic."

"Fine. Is this number on my cell OK?"

"That'll do."

"Bye."

My feelings toward Newark airport are representative of my feelings about the rest of New Jersey. What once was an accommodating place grew unfamiliar and unfriendly. I guess that happens with age. I used to go to the bars and feel like I knew everyone. I was comfortable. After awhile, I felt as if the transplants and newly-of-age leered at me as if I was the outsider. Newark International stirred that same feeling of estrangement. Shortly after the Oklahoma City bombing, they built these huge concrete barriers, hampering the ease of picking up arrivals. Then they closed the garage area to traffic altogether. After 9/11, no more walking down to the gates and waiting for your friends and family in a spacious seating area. People now stand awkwardly around the railings, unsure of what gate they should be keeping an eye on, again, feeling unwanted—just like I did in my own hometown. The message is clear: "We don't wanna get friendly with you; just use our service and scram."

I use EWR's service, to include car rental, and scram.

You would like Brocco. He reminds me of the DA from *Law and Order*, you know, the one who was a genuine senator. His droopy eyes and baritone voice suggest an empathy that contradicts the severity of his words. His true demeanor is unsympathetic. He is not happy about needing me to explain the message.

"I don't like this one bit," he says.

What the fuck does he want me to do about it?

"Well, there it is." He points to a note pad, the kind mailed from some

47

insurance agency, thanking new clients for being forced to give them their hard-earned money as dictated by the state.

I read the calligraphy-like penmanship: *Investigators, please contact Hattie Shore.* Followed by my cell phone number. *I began this, but I did not cause this. I am not to blame but to acknowledge. Your search is futile, but I am within reach. The irony is absurd.*

Fuck if he's not right about one thing: The irony *is* absurd. I imagine you're just as in the dark as the fake senator. It's not your fault, really. I've been holding back. I want to let you decide for yourself. Besides, I gotta tell ya, I really don't trust you either. If you are still here fifty pages from now, I may chance confiding in you. Until then, our relationship is gonna have to remain one-sided. You have to admit, there isn't much I can learn from you. In some ways, I'm all give, and you're all take. We don't need to apologize to each other. That's just the way it is.

"Are you going to let me in on the meaning of all this?"

The fake senator, might be a jerk—I'm not sure. "Where's the body?" I ask.

"Listen, I called you here as a courtesy. And I am in the *need-to-know.*"

I throw him a bone. "Does this case wrap up nicely if it weren't for the note?"

"Well … if not for the note, this would be a clear-cut suicide." As I pause to think, he becomes impatient. "Are you gonna let me in on this or what?"

"Can I see the body?"

Brocco begrudgingly leads me to the cadaver. Slit his wrists and sat down to watch TV. Cartoon channel.

"Can't really see any sign of foul play. Of course we'll have to wait for the tox screen to come back. But aside from being drugged, how does one successfully stage this kind of suicide?"

"It's not staged. He killed himself."

"But the letter?"

"I don't know. He's never communicated with me before."

"Who?"

I shake my head, ready for the tirade. "You're not gonna believe me."
I could tell him, but I'm sick of being ridiculed. "I'd prefer to mail you
my file and let you read it when I'm not around."

"I'm afraid that's not good enough," he says. "We can hold you and
compel you to explain."

No tirade. In fact, I sense wiggle room, so I ignore the threat. "I'll
mail you my file. You'll see I'm not interfering or holding back anything
you'll find pertinent to this case." *Because, unfortunately, you're probably
just like the rest of them.*

Truth is, I have no way of knowing when I will mail him my file. If
you, the reader, put this book down for a month, Brocco won't get my
notes for a while yet. Don't worry, I'm not obligating you to plod through;
I could really give a shit if he gets my file in a timely fashion.

"I'm a little fuzzy on who you are working for," he probes, sorta like
when one says, "What was your name again?" though you never told him
it to begin with.

"It's a personal pursuit—unfinished business from when I was on
the force."

"I heard about guys like you," says Brocco. At first, I thought he was
going to call me a *crackpot*. "Some cases you just got to let go. You can't
spend your retirement trying to meet every promise you make to yourself. At some point, you gotta live your life."

I was wrong. He is capable of empathy.

I nod and leave before he changes his mind and arrests me.

So now what? I guess you can follow me around, but that would get
old for you. I'm not a very good host—tour guide—whatever. No shit,
huh? You might as well return to the military story. Maybe you were even
into it. Things there seem to be back to normal. I suspect we'll meet
again.

Chapter Eleven

"Was that Father Atkinson?" asked Kick, gesturing with his cover in the direction of the whitewashed church.

"I wasn't looking," said the Corporal.

"I'll check," said Kick. "Hang out here in case the doc finishes before I get back. ... two birds with one stone. Not a bad day's work, heh?"

"Not at all, sir."

Kick jogged over to the church and tapped his right boot against the entryway frame as if he were knocking the dirt off his shoes—a quasi-knock—and entered the structure. The many windows illuminated the sanctuary, and Kick easily spied Atkinson ambling down the pews.

"Father Atkinson?" he called.

The priest turned.

"Yes, hello?"

Kick introduced himself and went into his *elevator spiel* about civil affairs, making sure to include "winning the hearts and minds of the people." The father was thrilled to finally meet a soldier who considered the people anything other than a logistical annoyance.

The two men continued their mutually praiseful conversation while joining up with Silas and the Corporal outside the clinic. Wendy, Silas' assistant, had arrived and took over the patient care while the four men talked outside. Together, they edited and added to Kick's list of *people-of-influence*. Kick took notes while the group discerned the community gripes. His plan involved getting the town's *key people* to meet the two units' key people so regular lines of communication could be established.

The goal was to set up hours of operation at the C-MOC for legal issues and initial medical triaging and psychological evaluation. The night the Corporal was summoned to the *head-shed* to meet the two CA officers, they had just finished *informing* the commanding officer of his responsibility to the host town, and that it was appropriate to handle JAG issues, individual medical cases, and even to allow screened nationals, especially NGO workers, onto the compound. This was all news to the colonel, who was more than happy to be told what he could do—even from lighter brass—rather than to fret over tangent issues. The colonel was more concerned with his primary mission, which, so far, only he, S-2, and the CA team were privy to here—though everyone else sensed it.

First, the CO was to set up and secure the MASH unit in time for the Cortinian president's return. Done. Next, he was to prepare for the large-scale vaccination effort that would commence once the president was in place. Possibly, the colonel's troops would be called on to assist in other relief efforts such as food dispersal. Ultimately, his primary objective was to "be ready."

The camouflage of a humanitarian effort was ideal for pre-staging a MASH and supporting units that would be essential should the presidential return not be accepted with open arms. Should American personnel come under fire, should there be a coup, the colonel was to "be ready."

So, this was why the colonel's unit appeared to be a contradiction—too busy working on humanitarian orders to take time to heal and recompense villagers. It was here as part of a contingency plan—it's present operations were essential only to maintain the appearance of care. The politicians justified this by assuming any aid is good aid; just as long as the MASH unit did not overextend itself and compromise its ability to treat U.S. personnel and Cortinian VIPs.

The colonel was glad for the CA team, as there were so many issues he didn't know how to address. *Are they even allowed to feed individual people? Do they chase off squatters? What if the police want to come on the compound?*

Upon the camp's initial setup, the man who owned the land, wanted access. The gate guards ushered him off under rifles. *What should they have done? Let the State Department sort out that crap.* It was easiest to have a policy of "no one in; no one out." Yes, the Corporal and his captain had free reign, but the colonel relied on the Marines to be appropriate.

In the colonel's favor, the one time an American NGO walked up to the compound's guards and asked to have a gash on his arm tended to, instead of turning him away or sending a doctor to stitch the guy up outside, the colonel actually allowed him to be treated inside the MASH compound. The colonel wasn't heartless; he just knew if the doctors began services with the villagers, it would get out of hand, and possibly jeopardize his primary mission. The potential care for American soldiers came first.

Now, the civil affairs personnel were here. They specialized in all these exigencies. Next time a villager wanders to the gate with a demand, the CO can pass it off to the CA team. It was a relief.

In two days, the Army key people would sit down with the civilian key people. Silas and Atkinson agreed to gather the local police representatives, the respected elders and other *people of influence.*

Kick needed to convince idle military personnel it was their job to establish relations with these people. But Kick had higher brass too. If he must, he could get his colonel stateside to lean on the appropriate people, but there was no need for a *pissing match*, especially when he knew the MASH CO was happy for the CA presence. There would be hemming and hawing, but in the end, JAG and the medical team reps would be present.

Fortunately, there was the S-1 officer, Franklin. He was gung-ho, can-do. He would be a great asset. Kick knew all he had to do was tell Franklin what he needed and it would be done. Franklin loved the military and the potential for good it could do. He reveled in the concepts of civil affairs. Back in the States, Americans' idea of the military was the *shock and awe* of its destructive prowess. Few even knew there was a proactive unit—a unit that deployed to countries in Africa's and Eurasia's poverty stricken depths to help build permanent infrastructure. Specialists were deployed to build waterworks, electrical systems, police forces, and such. This was Franklin's military. Unfortunately, it was the less publicized one; so much so, even Franklin didn't know of its existence when he upped, or else he would have joined the unit himself.

For Kick, S-2 was his greatest concern. Intelligence had very little to gain from the two-way interaction. They preferred one-way dialogue. Candid military dialogue only created a security threat. But Kick already had that covered. Though it was against CA policy to pump nationals for intelligence, there was no crime in stumbling across information and passing it on to S-2. Already, in the conversation with Atkinson, Kick learned of a problem with the water treatment facility, a possible contamination. He had also been tipped to a newly discovered mined road. Both pieces of information would be important to the S-2 officer. Kick would stretch the rules of intelligence-gathering to get S-2 to acquiesce when the need arose.

As they strode down the dirt road back to the MASH unit, the Corporal welled with the pride of the productive. He had a newfound respect for Kick. The lieutenant had handled himself quite professionally. The Corporal, like Franklin, had room for an amended appreciation of the American military, one honoring civil affairs' doctrine.

"When we get back, I would like to do a story on you, sir, if that is all right?" said the Corporal.

"Oh," hemmed Kick. "We'll see about that."

Again, there was that distrust of the press. Even someone as astute as Kick didn't understand the Corporal knew better than to print security sensitive material. For instance, the Corporal was not going to write about the contamination of the water-holds or the discovery of a mined road. Even if he had a *brain-fart*, the PAO would nix the stories upon review. The only way the Corporal could err would be to mail his story to an outside source. Then, he would be brought up on charges, having erroneously acted on behalf of the military and his CO.

Like many others, Kick didn't realize there is no investigative journalism in the military. The public affairs reporters are voices of the CO. The Corporal didn't write stories on the overshooting of a runway at Beaufort Air Station, but rather the new policies installed to prevent such case from happening again.

Yet, the Corporal felt forgiving. After all, he himself had known nothing about civil affairs until Kick and the major surfaced.

"How about if I have you read it first, so we don't print anything of a sensitive nature?" offered the Corporal. "I sure would like to let the people in the States know about the job you guys are going to do here."

Those were the words Kick needed to hear. "Yeah, that might work. Of course, you'll have to include the major, too. Though, I don't suppose there is any harm in you making me the hero of the story, right, Corporal?"

"No, sir. No harm at all."

The Corporal considered only a handful of people back home to be friends. Those dearest to him were the ones hardest earned. For some reason, the relationships that began abrasively always became the most solid. Perhaps he distrusted those who were too quick to make friends with everyone. There was something to be said for having to prove your mettle. Conversely, this hump back to the base was a good indicator for Kick as to the Corporal's character as well. The lieutenant appreciated a good double-time pace. The Corporal was no whiner. He was made of the same stuff as the lieutenant. Not all Marines were made of *blood and guts*, but those who were, gravitated toward each other and put the face they wanted on the Corps. Not only did the Corporal and lieutenant's Corps *not bitch*, it actually favored double-time—preferably in the rain and mud with a loaded rucksack, while the soldiers drove by in a feet-soothing caravan and howled their encouragement. *No sense in being a Marine if you didn't show off a little, right?*

Chapter Twelve

The Corporal sat on a crate, writing his story on a notepad, fearful of all the spelling errors otherwise flagged by a computer's spell-check. A laptop computer would have been too cumbersome and, worse yet, too fragile for his bang-it-into-a-duffle-bag mentality. *Who needed to worry about equipment that could break?* Yes, he fretted over his camera, but at least it wasn't his new digital body. For news print, six megs was enough. The pixilated black-and-white images of his paper hardly merited anything bigger. Besides, the smaller the images, the easier to send them over the lines.

Originally, the Corporal had planned on just taking notes and writing all the stories once he returned to the Air Station. Timeliness was never a big concern of the military press. Though they acted like they printed cutting news, in truth, delaying a story always ensured operational security. Military reporters didn't write about the upcoming mission but the mission's return and successes. That's why AP reporters rarely chummed around with the PAO's community relations representatives. If they waited on the liaison to keep them apprised of a story, it would be too late for the real world.

For smaller local news, most pictures were staged for the journalist, a practice justified by the notion the famous raising of the flag over Mount Suribachi was also a staged shot. If it was good enough for the most famous Marine Corps photo, it was good enough for the hometown gazette.

The Corporal recognized the CA story here warranted different treatment. The one on his own captain would be conclusive and could be written soon after the slated parade. The story on the CA efforts would be ongoing, as the mission had no culminating event, but rather individual successes. For once, the Corporal felt encouraged by a sense of timeliness, even novelty. He couldn't remember ever reading stories about the U.S. military anywhere not involving direct or potential conflict.

Once finished, the Corporal would type his story on Franklin's laptop—the Army was moved by caravan and had no difficulty shipping desks, copiers, computers and many other workplace comforts. After spell-checking his piece, the Corporal would transmit it home along with some pictures and their respective cutlines. Though Franklin wouldn't have complained, the Corporal wrote the story out by hand first to avoid monopolizing the computer and feeling pressured to settle on inferior writing in lieu of mulling over his sentences. Often, he would spend thirty minutes writing a lead. Unlike what high-school students are taught, reporters put the gist up front, under the notion a reader's attention span is limited. The writer presents the meat in an inverted pyramid of essentials. This aspect of news writing—the lack of a preamble—appealed most to the Corporal. He had never understood why the intent of a story in a school paper was defined in the last line of the first paragraph and not right up front, as if the student was gathering his thoughts.

Truly good writing should seem incidental, like the oil's value on a door without a squeak. The readers should become so enveloped in concision of reason, description, or dialogue they wouldn't take time to marvel over the writing concept. Good writing shouldn't squeak either.

On the other end of the line, another corporal would receive the

Ara 13

story, print, edit, and offer it for review by the gunnery sergeant, who wouldn't read it but rather sit with it, daydreaming in his office with his door closed for twenty minutes, emerge with the text in his hands, having incorrectly marked a few red-ink notations, falsely inserting commas or synonyms where inappropriate—though not a bad effort for never reading a sentence of the piece—and kick it back to the editing corporal with the verbal acknowledgement of "Good one, Devil Dog." For the gunny, the only use of the paper was to line the bottoms of bird cages. Perhaps he was right, but for those who didn't yet find futility in military reporting, the gunny's pretense of his underlings' importance was a transparent sham. Upon reflection, the Corporal had to admit that the gunny better realized Plato's allegorical cave shadows, thus insulating himself from taking life too seriously. However, the gunny's lethargic jadedness only fueled the notion the Corps was really run by the lower NCOs. Perhaps, it was just youth being more eager and ideal.

Fortunately, the gunny wasn't the last line of defense for what made it into print, grammatically or contextually. Once the editor made the gunny's changes, the editor reprinted it and sent it up to the public affairs officer for review. In this case, the officer was a very capable Chief Warrant Officer-4 who knew both grammar and correctness. Nothing but parody eluded him. Once, the Corporal had written a feature in the vernacular of a gumshoe which fell dead at the CWO-4's desk.

The CWO-4, whose ear was finely attuned to the frequency of the CO, knew instinctively what should go into print and what shouldn't. He also had an uncanny knack for finding all the added commas made by the gunny and striking them out.

Once the pages were laid out, the CWO-4 would review them again—a final front against grammatical and contextual incorrectness. Only a story like this one about the CA team overseas gave the CWO-4 pause. He didn't instinctively know what to do other than take a step back and consider.

The CWO-4 walked into the newsroom holding the copy and approached the editor. Day-to-day interaction among the enlisted correspondents and officers forgave the need for formalities such as popping to attention, or else the editing corporal would be jumping up every two seconds as officers milled in and out of his cubicle, dropping off announcements and such for print. Of course, if the CO or XO entered, "Attention on deck," would be commanded.

The editing corporal waited as the CWO-4 hesitated over him, dangling the copy and weighing the words in his mind like a politician practiced in the art of "we can neither confirm nor deny the presence of nuclear weapons"-speech.

"This piece—on the CA team ..." The CWO-4 pumped the paper up and down with deliberation as if weighing it for acceptability.

The editing corporal waited slack-jawed, mainly from the newly inserted and much too big tobacco wad pinched between his cheeks. He was used to this hesitant consideration of word choice in the CWO-4.

The officer looked up and made eye contact to emphasize his words. "It's good. No doubt about that ... it's good. But can we print it?" It was a rhetorical question posited as a display of the magnitude of thought gone into the answer.

"I want you to put a hold on this story for a bit until I can make a few phone calls and ensure we aren't stepping on anybody's toes, so to speak."

"Yes, sir. Sir, we do have the go ahead from the L-T and major—the two civil affairs officers on the ground. It would appear they OK'd it on their end." The corporal, of course, left room for the need for the CWO-4 to establish whether it was OK'd on his end. The editing corporal was smart enough to know where his opinion bordered on hubris of rank.

"Hmm"—a display of consideration for the corporal's benefit. The CWO-4 was always good enough to at least feign seeing the merit of his staff's opinion, again, so long as they didn't overstep their boundaries. The combat correspondents rarely did. They dealt with too much brass not to have learned *when to pull back their hands from the dogs' mouths*.

"Just the same, couch it for now."

"Yes, sir."

Chapter Thirteen

Three well-dressed civilians were causing a ruckus at the MASH gate. Major Johnson was summoned from his tent to address the interlopers. As he approached, he spied two native men and an American woman. The woman, wielding a clipboard like an all-access pass, agitatedly spoke with her arms flailing about her. As Johnson approached, he recognized a British accent, perhaps South African.

The major walked out the gate, past the Army guard who stood imposing his armed authority between the civilians and the entrance, and gave a warm greeting from behind a plastered smile. "Hi, you all. I'm Major Johnson. How can I be of assistance?"

"Well, for starters," began the woman, "you can let us on base so we can inspect the facility." Her irritation caused her to begin with her demand instead of her credentials. She realized her omission when the corners of the major's smile sagged in confusion.

"I'm Drew Lange, and I am with the Cortinia environmental agency. From here, I can see oil from those trucks leaking onto the ground," she said, pointing with her clipboard.

Johnson turned to regard the large vehicles of motor-T, under which pieces of torn cardboard were haphazardly staged to catch leaking fluid. The major nodded his head in agreement.

"And what else are your concerns?"

"Standing water. As you probably know, disease comes easy here."

The major smiled again at Drew and suppressed his impulse to immediately invite them onto the compound. He would run it by the colonel first.

"I'm sorry if you've already been made to wait, but I must ask you for just a little more patience while I clear this with the colonel. Can I borrow your identification cards for a moment please?"

"You're coming right back?" she asked reproachfully.

"Right back. I won't disappear on you."

Johnson smiled at the specialist on guard duty—his way of reminding the guard *this is a friendly environment.* He entered the compound and headed for the TOC, considering the implications of the tour from the eyes of the CO.

Drew turned to her two assistants. "This is fucking bullshit," she said under her breath; and she gave an accusing leer at the guard. In no way was she prepared for the reception that followed minutes later. Johnson returned with an eager captain.

"Drew Lange, gentlemen, this is Captain Snider, our unit environmental officer. He and I would be glad to give you a tour of the facility."

"Alex," said the captain as he extended his hand to Drew. Drew stared at his hand, more amazed over the welcome than insulted by the breach of island customs. The major, smiling all the while, lowered the confused captain's outstretched arm and talked away the faux pas.

"We are most interested in correcting any violations," he said.

"I can see the problem with the oil, and we will get pans for under the trucks," said Snider, taking the major's lead. "Until they arrive, we must be more diligent with the placement of cardboard. As for standing water, there are only the waterbulls and the large bladders for the showers, and they are enclosed. Come, I'll show you."

Drew and the two assistants, somewhat stunned, followed the soldiers through the gate and onto the compound. By the end of the tour, Drew, the major, and the captain were so chummy, Drew didn't even notice she was steered around the TOC, equipment shed and armory—the only objections S-2 could come up with.

Drew and Snider exchanged contact numbers; and the captain was so pleased to be performing real-world environmentalism he needed somebody's hand to shake. He settled for an enthusiastic good-bye shake with the two male assistants and bade them all "Godspeed." Having won the hearts and minds of three people, Johnson beamed as if he just finessed a war victory and not an acquiescence of dusty, cardboard pan substitutes.

Chapter Fourteen

Franklin received the Corporal's e-mail from stateside and summoned the Marine without snooping at his letter.

"Attention on deck. Marine on deck!"

"Cut it out," said Franklin to the TOC guard, discouraging the guard's diversion from serious duty. The Corporal approached the lieutenant and popped to his modified position of attention, which Franklin quickly eschewed.

"Just double-click on it Devil Dog," he said, offering up his laptop. "Let me know when you're through. Believe it or not, I actually have some work to get to."

"Yes, sir. I won't be but a moment. Thank you, sir." The Corporal launched the letter from back home:

Sorry, buddy. The gunner put your story on hold. I'm not sure if he has the balls to print it. (If you are not supposed to be reading this, it is a federal crime to look through someone else's mail, via internet or post—it's in the UCMJ. Look it up!)

The Corporal smiled. His editor was just screwing around. He would never have documentarily questioned his CWO-4's virility if the Corporal hadn't vouched for Franklin's discretion with the assuring words, "he's cool."

The Corporal considered his response. He had been aware of this possibility, and he knew the next step to take, but he wasn't sure if he wanted to take it. "What the hell," he thought. He took comfort knowing he was not going to violate any laws. He was merely working the system. He wrote:

Don't tell the gunner you talked with me. Find the name of the military paper at Fort Dix, New Jersey. Ensure it is run by the military and not civilians; and get me an e-mail address. As far as you know, I sent you and them the copy simultaneously. Since the major and L-T are from Dix, the copy is newsworthy; and as long as the paper is run by the military, we COAes. If they print it, the onus is on them to ensure its classification. Besides, they would know best. I'll check back in twenty. O-R D.D. Remember, I never suspected it wouldn't go to print since it was OK'd here, but don't bring it up until it is in the Dix paper. I already deleted your message.

The editor did his job, and twenty minutes later, the Corporal returned to the TOC and borrowed Franklin's laptop to check his e-mail.

One minute later, the Corporal's story was shotgunned to Dix's *The Post*. One week later, the editor knocked on his CWO-4's open door, came to his own modified position of attention until his PAO looked up and told him to enter.

"Sir," began the corporal. "I just received a second installment from Cortinia on that story we were considering." The editor could pick the right words when need be.

"Oh" the CWO-4 hedged. "Yeah, I'm still hesitant."

"Yes, sir," said the editing corporal. Then, he steeled himself for the sneak attack. He tried to continue as matter-of-factly as possible. "Although, the first story did get printed in Fort Dix's military paper. It seems he sent it to both of us since the CA officers are from the 404th. He did it as a courtesy not knowing we would hold it, but I told him not to send them another installment until you give the *go ahead*."

The CWO-4 sat forward, clasped his hands together and stared down at them. He pumped his hands as he spoke, controlled and calculating. "And they are a military paper run by the PAO of Dix?" He looked up, emphasizing the need for precision.

"Yes, sir. They signed off on the printing of their own mission."

The CWO-4 nodded his head. "This could be a good thing. If they're fine with it, there is no reason why we shouldn't be, right?"

Again, it was the CWO-4's habit to ask rhetorical questions under the guise of inclusion.

But the corporal jumped at the opening. "Yes, sir. In fact, we can ensure the story is in print by them first and choose the same editing as theirs before we go to print with it."

Only in the military is being scooped a good thing.

"I think that's a plan," said the CWO-4. "But I want to see the edited version that goes into print from Dix. Straight from their paper, not e-mail."

"Yes, sir." *Now, for phase two:* "Sir, after we go to print, can I send it out for release?"

"After we go to print," agreed the CWO-4, acting as if there remained some integrity in being second to print.

"Yes, sir."

From then on, the Corporal's CA stories appeared in Dix's *The Post*, then a week later at Beaufort Air Station, and a week to three after that in military papers up and down the eastern seaboard, in California, in *Stars and Stripes* and *Leatherneck*, and even sometimes in New Jersey's *The Star Ledger*, though most civilian papers didn't see the newsworthiness of proactive military actions overseas. After all, no one from the Garden State was getting killed. They were merely doing good.

With the publication of the CA stories, Kick greatly warmed up to the Corporal. It became Kick's habit to summon the Corporal prior to performing any CA work. He even became the Marine's surrogate officer, in light of his captain's continuing absence. The Corporal was unsure how much longer he would be in-country as the parade was scheduled to happen within seven weeks; however, he gleaned the real reason for his captain's presence—as an interpreter during interrogations—might keep him here longer. Either way, the captain would decide his fate.

Kick got the Corporal access to his *own* laptop, which was staged in the TOC on a table top—not quite a desk—with a placard reading *Public Affairs.*

Two NCOs arrived to join the increasingly busy CA team. With them came a jeep, making the hump into town a thing of the past. In two months, the CA team established a civilian post office, a work-program with a credible labor organization, and communication lines to forestry services, water, and gas reps, as well as a strengthened relationship with local medical and law enforcement services.

The systems were so well in place, the CA NCOs could summon the often-lethargic local authorities to respond to any outside-the-gate disturbances without having to convince them of their duty. The local police would arrive, handle the disruptor, and leave. The town's medical groups were just as responsive. Unless an individual had an immediate threat to *life or limb*, villagers were referred to the local medical facility, which was augmented by military personnel and some supplies. This created an air of habituation, keeping stragglers away from the compound and fostering a relationship with the locals and their home facilities. Of course, if an individual was gravely hurt near the compound, after a security and body check, he would be taken inside the gate and treated. The smoothness of protocol was confirmed after one woman, who had a fatal embolism, was accepted onto the compound for treatment before succumbing to her condition. The local authorities didn't even question the good intentions of the MASH unit's command. Prior to the CA's arrival, a national's death on the compound could have spurred a misguided village riot.

Even S-2 was happy. Intelligence received periodic reports on potential insurgent activities, though usually diffused by Silas, Atkinson, and the CA team. S-2's gate guards were also less often accosted by villagers bringing random findings—vehicle parts and such—potentially taken for pipe bombs, creating an unnecessary rise in *alert*. With the ease in tension, the gate guards no longer threatened the occasional well-meaning visiting villagers, but referred them to the C-MOC or sometimes even the appropriate local agency. They were proud to know the correct recommendation.

Slowly, the idea of assisting the nation permeated the minds of the soldiers who interacted with the nation's people. Perhaps, the U.S. military really could win the hearts and minds of the people. The military personnel seemed to move from treating the villagers as toddlers—scolding them before they reached for the oven burners—to regarding them as preteens, explaining why they were being denied an activity. Still, though, the military didn't look upon the nationals as adults. But, the troops were less inclined to call them *gooks* and behave as xenophobic, spoiled heirs, indignantly marking time, offended by the expectation that they perform their contractual duty in return for the G.I. Bill.

Occasionally, the new, helpfulness backfired. If a well-intentioned soldier suggested a possible avenue of assistance, the villager sometimes took it as a promise. One day, a CA soldier told a villager there might be work in the future—to "try again next week." The villager returned with seven others, all demanding the military make good on its promise for employment. Because of incidents such as this, soldiers learned not to insinuate help they had only a chance of providing. In short, they removed *maybe* from their vocabulary and relearned how to say *no* instead of speculating on possibilities. Until one knew for certain, a *no* was wisest while one shored up avenues of assistance.

Silas and Kick drove up to the MASH front gate and sent for the Corporal. When the Corporal arrived, the two men had removed an old bicycle from the back of the vehicle. Days before, the Corporal had assisted a villager by unloading his rickety old truck. The villager associated the

Corporal with the CA team, and to show his appreciation—and to stay in the good graces of the CA unit—he wanted to give him a bike, no longer used by his son, who was now working away from the village.

"I can't accept that. That's too much from him," said the Corporal.

"Look at it as a loan," said Silas. "It was a major thing for him to gift it. You can't turn it down. But you can return it before you go back stateside. We'll tell him the military wouldn't let you take it with you."

"Can I give him anything in return?"

"I already gave him the candy out of my MRE," said Kick half-joking. "He seemed good with that."

The Corporal looked at the old, black bike with its big wicker basket and a bell; and he smiled. He would never be caught dead on a bike such as this in the States, but here, he knew, it would make him a star. He had only seen a few bicycles in Cortinia, and certainly none carrying a military member. The Corporal mounted the bike, rode it through the gate and onto the compound. "Thank you, gentlemen," he said and rang the bell. Kick and Silas laughed. Several soldiers, while moving out of the way, heeding the bell's warning, did a double-take.

"Hey, Marine, where did you get the bike?"

"In town. I got it for a pack of M&Ms."

"Fucking cool."

He rode the bike among the open-flapped tents, soaking up attention. The soldiers gawked or cheered, depending on how the oddity struck them. As he rounded the armory, a lieutenant he hadn't met yelled to him, "Soldier, get over here!" but the Corporal didn't realize he was being addressed. The lieutenant ran up to the Marine and grabbed his right handlebar from behind. The Corporal looked back annoyed as he almost toppled over, but he saw the muted bars and retained his bearing.

"Yes, sir?" he asked, as he recovered his footing. He didn't recognize the name tape—*Mills*.

"How about coming to a position of attention and saluting, soldier."

"Yes, sir." The Corporal knew to agree before dissenting. "We don't salute in the box, sir; CO's orders. And I'm a Marine, sir."

"W ... What?" the lieutenant stammered.

"I'm not a soldier, sir. I'm a Marine," he said, feeling awkward standing at attention with a bike leaning against him.

The lieutenant was new to the box. Still, he was typical of a butter-bar officer when faced with something out of the ordinary—order first, think second.

"Who's your commander?"

"Colonel Smith, sir," he said. The CO wasn't really his colonel, but he knew the whole explanation about his attachment would only confuse the issue. The lieutenant kept the Corporal at attention while he thought.

"Let's go there. Walk the bike."

"Yes, sir."

Several soldiers stared as the Corporal walked by, escorted by the lieutenant, as if the young NCO were a cattle rustler, walking the horse that would later depart out from under him, leaving him dangling in a noose hung from a tree limb. In front of the TOC, the Corporal lowered the kickstand and staged his bike. He unzipped the tent's flap, and the lieutenant followed him inside. Once there, the guard behind the desk came to attention. Mills was confused when the sergeant announced, "Attention on deck; Marine on deck!" and then merely acknowledged the lieutenant with a nod and a hello-like "Sir."

Before Mills could decide whether or not to admonish the sergeant, Franklin approached jovially.

"Corporal, how's it going today?"

"Great, sir. And you?"

Mills tried to change the tone of the dialogue. "Lieutenant, I found this soldier riding around ..." but Franklin cut him off.

"Marine. He's a Marine not a solider. You don't want to keep making that mistake if you want to live to talk about it," he joked, not noticing the lieutenant was attempting to report an incident.

"I got a bike, sir," said the Corporal.

Franklin inhaled as if he just heard of the best Christmas gift in the world. "You got a bike? Let me see." He proceeded out the tent, leaving Mills awkwardly behind.

"Wow, that's great," he sang, holding the bike's handlebars. "Can I ride it?"

The Corporal chuckled. "Yes, sir."

Franklin saddled the bike, began peddling and whooped and smiled, careening around in fast circles. He slid to a halt right in front of the Corporal and lieutenant. "Where did you get it?" he asked, still smiling wide.

"In town, for a bag of M&Ms."

"You got to be kidding me," he overly enunciated.

"No, sir," replied the Corporal, playing on the mysteries of being allowed outside the box.

"That's great," said Franklin as he handed the bike over to the Corporal. "Cool, huh?" he said to Mills, expecting him to join in staring at the raggedy old bike as if it were the newest car out of production.

"Then it's OK?" asked Mills.

"What?" responded Franklin, still having no idea the lieutenant's intent had been to dress-down the Marine. Then, Franklin's role as operations officer occurred to him. "Mills? Are you new? I don't think I have you in the system. Come, you can't be avoiding work just because we don't know you are here," he said and unzipped the TOC flap.

Mills turned to see if the Marine had overheard the semi-jesting chastisement, but the Marine was good enough to at least pretend he was giving his full attention to the bike's pedals.

"Gentlemen," said the Corporal as he popped to attention, recognizing the officer's departure.

"Cut that shit out," said Franklin. He shook his head, smiled conspiratorially at Mills, and chided, "Fucking Marines, eh?"

Chapter Fifteen

The Corporal kept his bike outside the guard's and his sleeping quarters. There was no need to lock it up; *where would anyone steal it to?* He knew better than to ride it outside the box. It would make him stand out too much from the other military personnel. He didn't mind standing out inside the box, where it was mostly taken in awe and good humor, but outside, in the real world, being conspicuous often brought trouble.

A helicopter flew by as the Corporal walked to chow. The soldiers in the compound stared up, uncertain what to make of the bird. They were so immersed in their area of expertise—the medical field—they often forgot other constituents of the military, like tanks and helicopters. In fact, most soldiers in the medical field were so green to infantry, they wouldn't have known if the copter was Russian or American. They did know it was the first copter they'd seen since setting up camp.

After chow, the Corporal and Kick drove into town to meet with Silas and update each other on their progress. The three men stood outside the expanded hospital when faint gun shots rose out of the northeast.

"Oh dear," said Silas.

Kick waited until the shots subsided, listening all the while as if he were deciphering Morse code. "Have you heard sustained shots like that before?" Kick asked Silas.

"Not in some time."

"Do you know of anything ...?" Kick trailed off, unsure how to ask about combat, without seeming inept.

"I'd tend to think that's a question I should ask of you."

Kick nodded. He would see what he could learn from the colonel when they returned to the box.

The colonel knew nothing about the initial occurrence. But as the days passed, two more incidents were heard, still very far away. The colonel received little response from the other units. "Just one or two individual dissidents we finally located," said Colonel Habersham.

"Things just aren't the same," the Corporal told Kick, conversing among soldiers milling about outside the TOC.

"How so?" asked Kick.

"Before you came, sir, there used to be all kinds of peddlers on the roads. I'd get spooked on the days they were absent and the roads were quiet. Now, I'm used to their absence. I don't think that's a good thing."

He continued. "And there are certainly a lot more patrol units about town. I used to run into one every couple of days. Now, we see them drive by periodically. They know something's up. Damn infantry, they're either tight-lipped or exaggerating. I can't tell what's what. But something's up, sir."

Kick nodded. "There hasn't been any civilian mail posted in a couple of days," he added.

"What's that mean?"

"It's a barometer. We put the boxes a mild walk from town. The amount of mail lets us gauge the comfort level of the villagers. If there is little mail, then they don't feel comfortable wandering around outside their immediate area. It means the people know something is up too."

"You did that on purpose?"

"Just happened that way. We didn't have enough boxes so we staged them between two main settlements."

"I guess there's bound to be some armed resistance to the president's return, right?" asked the Corporal.

"Who knows?" said Kick. "Have you heard from your captain?" he added as if answering his first question.

"He just shoots Lieutenant Franklin a line every now and then to check up on me. It's purely one-way communication. He'll have the L-T assist me if I need anything, but I haven't seen my captain in weeks."

"Must be the new Corps," said Kick, not liking how the captain seemingly abandoned his Marine.

"I know it might not look good, sir, but the captain was good enough to take me with him. Believe me, it's worlds better than the bullshit we were doing back home."

"Yeah, now you're saving the world, right Corporal?"

They grew silent as another helicopter buzzed by overhead. Several soldiers stared up, but many just kept about their business, as if two of anything abnormal was enough for it to become commonplace.

"Perhaps, that's another barometer. Maybe the mailbox ..." The Corporal's words are overcome by a large explosion from the east side of the compound. Ground debris and gate shoot into the air nearly in unison with a concussing boom. From the woods, a dozen or so guerrillas run to the hole in the perimeter, firing full burst onto the compound.

"WHAT THE FUCK, WHAT THE FUCK, WHAT THE FUCK!" the Corporal yells.

I drop my clipboard, take off my cover, and emerge from a crowd of gawking soldiers.

"This is not my fault," I say apologetically. "I followed *him* in here again."

"You can't do this now; we are at a major plot development!" replies the Corporal.

"I know, I know ... the tensions are escalating. Well, here they are,"

I say, gesturing toward the breaching guerillas, trying to harvest humor in chaos.

"No, it's much too early!" yells Kick.

"I'm sorry, I thought I could get in and out without anyone noticing."

"Do you know what happened last time!" the Corporal admonishes. "*He* had me shot in the fucking head! I was just standing there, giving my lines, and out of nowhere, *bammo*, a bullet pierces my fucking skull. It took me an hour to die. It was fucking bullshit! I'm the goddamn protagonist of this fucking story. I'm not supposed to get shot in the fucking head!"

"Can't you leave us alone," whines Kick. "Ara wrote us back alive once already. I doubt he'll do it a second time. He'll probably just give up on us."

Franklin pops his head out from the TOC. I see several soldiers beyond him holding onto their desks with both hands as if the *big one* were coming. "This isn't in the script," he says confused.

Soldiers are scurrying about. Some gather their bearings and begin firing back at the guerrillas. Several others go about their day-to-day as if nothing is happening. Two officers are having a casual conversation a short distance from the breach. One of them gets mowed down in a hail of guerrilla gunfire. The other continues talking to the mangled mass until a guerrilla closes in on him and runs him through with a K-bar.

A private sprints by Franklin, stripped to his boots and attempting to adjust his gas mask while yelling, "We're in present tense! We're in present tense!"

Franklin watches the lunatic soldier, digesting the his words. "We *are* in present tense, aren't we?" A volley of bullets rip into Franklin's frame and he falls to the dirt. "But, I'm light comic relief," he says and passes.

Kick and the Corporal look to me panicked. Damn, I feel obligated.

"Come with me," I tell them. I run behind the armory, past the showers and toward the back gate.

"We can't go through there; it hasn't been swept for mines yet," warns the Corporal.

"They are just notional mines. Ara only wrote in people talking about the presence of the mines without needing to construct them. They're never to detonate in the story. He based the mined road on an exercise in Louisiana. They weren't real then either. You can't die from notional mines."

"Whatever, dude. Let's go," says a motivated soldier who has joined our small group.

"Who is this?" I ask.

"I don't know. He's just a minor character, probably falling under phrases like 'soldiers milling about.' Ara hasn't even given him a *name*," chides the Corporal.

"*You* don't have a name," I remind him.

"That's a literary device. He always capitalizes Corporal like it *is* my name. It's some sort of Jungian alter-ego."

The Corporal turns to the unnamed soldier. "Get out of here, will ya."

"To hell with you. I'm following him," he says, pointing at me.

"We can't just leave him here," says Kick.

"You guys don't have any say in the matter," the unnamed soldier declares. "As far as I'm concerned, there aren't any main characters anymore."

I grab the M16 from the unnamed soldier and pry up the razor wire so the others can low-crawl under it. On the other side, the unnamed soldier holds the wire up for me, and we four sprint down the back connector of the two camps.

"I'm not supposed to gain access to this connector yet," says the Corporal. "I have my big scene here."

"Then go back," suggests the unnamed soldier.

The Corporal peers over his shoulder at the devastation that once was the MASH compound, but he keeps pace with us. As we reach halfway to 432's gate, we are halted by a sentry off in the woods.

"Let me see your hands!" he yells.

"Can't you see the MASH unit is overrun?" cries the Corporal.

"Did you come from the shack in the woods?"

75

"What the fuck are you talking about?" responds Kick.

"He wants the password," says the unnamed soldier. "We have to respond using the password in a sentence."

"Can't you see the fucking fighting?" continues the Corporal.

"What's the password?" I ask.

"We don't know any damn password," says Kick. "It was never written into the story."

"Are you fucking crazy?" The Corporal is panicking. The sentry is beginning to bug out.

"Damn it," I mutter. "Come on." I sprint off into the woods and head south in a line tangent to the two camps. The sentry fires after us. I can hear the others follow suit. The unnamed soldier returns fire. Someone yells out in pain. I'm not going to get caught up in this mess. If they make it, they make it. At least the unnamed soldier has the presence of mind to return fire.

I run for about an hour or a line of text. The fighting is fainter, and the grunts of the men keeping pace behind me are more distant. I stop by a natural blind with a giant rock to the rear so I can monitor the two avenues of approach. The unnamed soldier arrives first.

"Kick's been hit. We should wait for him."

What the hell am I doing? This is ridiculous. I'm wasting time here … for what? But the unnamed soldier looks filially at me.

"How far back?" I ask.

"Not far; they kept pace most of the way."

"All right."

The Corporal arrives first, sweating bullets. He doubles over trying to catch his breath. Kick appears moments later. He is pale and clammy. His left arm rests limp at his side, and his shirt sleeve is soaked in blood from above his elbow down to the cuff. Once the adrenaline from the run wears off, the pain will really set in.

"You ready?" I ask.

"Wait," says Kick. The Corporal remains bent low to the ground. Only the unnamed soldier is game to continue.

"You gonna make it?" I ask, thinking it evident he will.

"No," says Kick.

"Well, you don't have much choice," I respond. "I've got to find the perimeter of the story." Kick is breathing heavy. I'm afraid the pain will incapacitate him before I can get him moving again.

"No, I do have a choice," he says and pulls the 9mm from his side holster.

"You can't shoot him," says the unnamed soldier, concerned for me. "He's our way out."

Kick chuckles. He points the gun at his own temple.

"Dude, wait," says the unnamed soldier, holding out his arms as if to stave off any sudden moves. The Corporal is seated motionless on the ground.

"I'm done," says Kick. I half-expected this.

"What do you mean you're done? We can do this," the unnamed soldier argues.

"What's the point? I'm in pain. It's only going to get worse. And who knows how I'll get it. At least, now, I can end it quickly and hope Ara doesn't give up on us." He turns to the Corporal. "See you when we get rewritten." We all flinch at the report. Kick keels over dead. I'm more worried about the sound of the gunshot being heard. And I don't know if the Corporal is going to skit out or what. Fuck, I don't need this.

"We should keep going," I say. I look to the unnamed soldier. He just blinks at me. I turn to continue.

"Fucking wait!" yells the Corporal. I hear a round being chambered. I turn to find him pointing his own 9mm at me. "I said wait," he reiterates, calming his voice. He's trying to get control of a hopeless situation. I look at him like I'm bored.

"So, how about you?" asks the Corporal.

"How about me what?"

The unnamed soldier is momentarily stunned into watching the events.

"We die, we suffer, we get rewritten. How about you? Can you die?"

"Not here. I'm above it."

"Why; 'cause you exist outside this stupid story?"

"Yes."

"But will it hurt?"

"It won't happen," I tell him.

"It will if I shoot you." I can tell he will.

"You can't."

"Let's find out."

"You don't understand. It just won't happen." I don't know why I'm trying to reason with him. He's nothing like the character he portrays. There isn't an ounce of competence or integrity in his body. The polarity is nearly humorous.

"What have I got to lose," he says.

Again, that damn loud report. We might as well send up smoke signals. The Corporal looks up at me from the ground. The gaping hole in the side of his face is nearly as large as the gawping hollow of his surprised mouth.

"That's easy for you, Marine!" yells the unnamed soldier, the M16 still in the crotch of his arm, the barrel covering the Corporal's dead body. "You're a main character. You'll get written back. But not me. I'm a 'soldier milling about.' That might be it for me. If it ends here, I probably won't return, you selfish prick."

"Let's go," I say.

The unnamed soldier gazes at me, emotionless. I don't want to be looking at him when his expression turns to one of shame. I'd rather not console characters.

We run through the woods for another, let's say, hour. Trees appear less frequently and seem to loop as if the same group is skipping like a record.

"What the hell?" says the unnamed soldier. He spies the occasional empty spots on the ground, the whiteness of nothing written, peering through the forest floor. I slow as we approach the clear white chasm. The unnamed soldier doesn't notice the chasm ahead, for he has nearly stopped progressing. He's spinning to stare at the blankness of that not written. I wait for him to sidle up next to me. I hardly have the energy for when he looks up. I don't want to explain the world to him. It's too much.

"Did you see all the ..." He shuts up and stares forward into the great unwritten whiteness. "Holy shit," he says quietly. "Now what?"

"I have to continue on."

"Can I come, too?"

"Give me your chevrons."

He slings his rifle and dutifully pops his chevrons from his collar. Don't ask me why I didn't want to take his canteen or anything else *important*. I guess I kind of like his character.

"Watch." I toss his chevrons into the great whiteness. They disappear. "They don't exist beyond here. Neither would you."

"That man you're after; he's in there?"

"Yes."

He considers his next question. "Is it Ara?"

"No."

He nods as if we had come to an agreement. Serene now, he meekly inquires, "Where are you going next?"

"Auschwitz."

PART TWO

Chapter One

Well reader, you might as well follow me since you've come this far. I'm not quite sure what you expect to get out of all this. Maybe you're just killing time. But you'll have to excuse me if I don't analyze your motives any further. I've got a job to do.

I don't know if you're ready for this. Hell, I don't know if I'm ready, but it's something I gotta do.

Before my eyes can adjust to the near darkness, I am overcome by the powerful stench. The *sleeping* bodies are so crammed together, they wouldn't fit if they weren't so emaciated. I don't think I'm going to continue to tell you what I see. I'd be a phony. It's one thing to narrate a conflict; it is another to pretend the insight necessary to express the horrors of a concentration camp. Besides, this story has been told by legitimate sources. It's not my place to try. One can't describe the reality of a horror he's never experienced—at least not without sobering guilt for the attempt. However, we don't have to experience the horror to empathize and reap the lesson—to consider the circumstances, to take personal inventory. Yes, it may be futile to ask *what we would do*, but still, we must wear the shoes, chance the hubris, attempt to foolishly consider the evil, and the circumstances—but perhaps this is best done in private. So, privately I digest my surroundings, I embrace the lesson, I carry on the memory. But I cease the attempt at description. It is not mine to describe beyond the audience of me.

He was through here; I'm sure.

"You there," whispers a voice.

I inch over to one of the talking skulls. I am speechless. What can one say to this man?

"I know why you are here."

I still have no words. I stare into the pools of his eyes. The life in his pupils belie the near death of his frame.

"He was here. I saw him."

"How do you know it was him?" I ask.

"Our powers of observation are heightened. We are attuned to every nuance. We must notice; It is life and death."

I nod. Words continue to fail me. I feel a coward, a phony for even relaying this part to you.

"You know, we too had a trial for him, in absentia of course." He spoke in a thick Semitic accent.

"And?"

"And ... and what's the point? We blame him; so? We do not get our lives back. But ..."

"But what?" I ask.

"But we never had him in front of us. We never accused him while looking into his eyes. Who knows what then?"

I wasn't sure if he meant he would be more forgiving or more inflamed. I suppose he meant different things for different people. Victims have various coping mechanisms. The guilt, the punishment—it's not my jurisdiction.

He reads my face and patiently waits until my inner dialogue ceases.

"The children's hospital, Mengele—you understand?"

I understand. I walk over to the so-called hospital. You might be wondering how I can move around so easily inside such a place—a realm of concertina wire, armed guards, dogs, and the like. Hell, you may even want to know how I can travel back to such a time. The answer is: the same way you can. Don't look at me like that. I'm no different than you. You can go anywhere you want to go in your mind. Where do you think we are now? I'm not sitting there beside you.

If you haven't taken the journey here yourself, shame on you. Who cares if it's cliché? It's necessary. How can you consider yourself humane if you yourself have never walked around history? Sometimes even fiction will do. Your world would be so small.

I'm sorry—I'm lashing out at you, unwarrantedly. My emotions are manifesting elsewhere as they are simultaneously suppressed, like a pocket of water that must bubble out somewhere when compressed.

I enter the children's ward. A diminutive girl beckons me over from her cot. These individuals know to look for me because I want to talk with them, to understand, to remember. I can't even offer the normal pleasantries. *How are you?*—an absurd question I'm unable to frame.

"I can tell you about him," she whispers.

I pull up a stool and lean into her soft words.

"He was here when they took my sister. We are twins. She is very sick. They injected her with some disease, but she refuses to die. She knows if she dies, they will kill me too to compare the bodies—to see what the sickness does. She stays alive for me."

"Does he intervene?" I ask, probing further than I need.

"He just observes."

I nod. I am ashamed for having felt in the past my life would be more inspirational if only it were more tragic. Again, I feel phony—a coward. I pat her hand, get up, and walk out the ward. Now, if you'll excuse me. I need time by myself ...

Ara 13

Displaced People

Hockney called me. He wanted to see how I am doing. He must have heard about the message for me in Manhattan from detective Brocco. I didn't give him any *I told you so's*. I just made small talk and wished him my best. I could still hear the skepticism in his voice, but he held back commenting. I doubt I'll ever fully win Hockney over. Who knows what barriers constructed in upbringing I would have to knock down for him to see the truth? Often, beliefs molded from childhood can only be fracture with a bolt of lightning. I'm not making a grand commentary on nurture. In fact, I think the whole nature/nurture dichotomy is a crock. But you can overcome *upbringing*. Reason can win out. Now, I don't know if that means one is activating the nature element—realizing potentials, and all. Fuck, I'm babbling again. I hate going into this shit. I usually avoid motives when pursuing people. Who cares about the *whys*, just as long as I find my quarry? But I keep hitting road blocks here.

It's been awhile since I looked at the profile. I get so caught up in pursuing this guy, I stop thinking about the person. He becomes a trail, not flesh and blood—hell, he may not even *be* flesh and blood for all I know. Lately, I feel as if I am merely documenting his whereabouts. I'm always one step behind him. Since I have yet to overtake him, I need to change my approach, but how in the world could I ever find somewhere he is *going to be*."

This is beyond my purview, you understand. I just want to bring him in, not to dissect him. But, sometimes to find someone, you have to try and understand his motives. This case isn't like a hit-and-run where all I have to do is follow up on some witness ID of the license plate, arrest the car's owner, and punch holes in his phony alibi. To nab the hit-and-runner, I don't have to understand what led him to driving fast in residential areas. Who cares if he is an egomaniac, the product of an abused childhood, recently dumped by his girlfriend, or just an aspiring Mario Andretti? That's for the lawyers and courts to sort out. When I was on the job, I cared only about locating the idiot and bringing him in. Sure, I had my theories, but they were just trivial gossip. My notes on the event would have only cursory value compared to the follow-up interviews of the lawyers and their subsequent spin. In the end, why someone did something was morphed, depending on the best defense, not the core truth.

Yet, for once, I am faced with delving into the *whys* of this guy on the lam just to try and gain a step on him. It would help if others weren't so blind to his existence—the ultimate irony if you ask me. I'm usually the pragmatic one, the skeptic of the group. It's quite unlike me to rely on gut feeling. Perhaps that's why I get caught up documenting his presence—for my own peace of mind. It helps me to know I'm not screwy. Though, I know the others still doubt the extent I say he is involved, I think you, the reader, may be coming around. Aren't you?

Here's the file—on my desk. You're welcome to it. It's a who's who of history. More accurately, it's a where's where. Rwanda, Normandy, Gettysburg, Leningrad. Then there are places you may not have even heard about. Small villages, small towns, small people. Knock yourself out. Read them all if you want. After awhile, they run into each other, tales of carnage: dead, dead, tortured, dead, raped, dead. And *he* was there.

You would investigate too. Who wouldn't? You'd run the same gamut of emotions as I did: horror, outrage, sadness, anger, depression, futility. Is futility an emotion? How's numbness? No, I can't quite say that either. You were there at Auschwitz; you know I wasn't impervious.

Why don't you look at the file later? Let's go mail that letter I promised the fake senator—you remember—Brocco. I said I would send him my notes on the case. I photocopied a handful of the smaller batches and left out most of my personal assessments, copying only the generic observations. Temporarily, that's enough to seem as if I had kept my word. Still, I lied to him. It won't reveal anything or make him understand the message left for me on his home turf. But, I promised to do it, and, more importantly, I like the fact *you* know my promise. Maybe we're bonding.

At the post office is a manila envelope for me. Hand written in large black marker on the envelope's front is *Hattie Shore*. No address, no return, no postage. Someone just stuck it in my box. I undo the small clasp. The envelope isn't sealed.

Hattie Shore,

There is no getting around it now. Here I am. Well, not really; this is just some pressed wood and rosin. In some sense, it is tree on tree. Do you like my handwriting? Immaculate?

I enjoy our game. As you know, I like to test people. I especially like that you abhor me, though that will cost you in the long-run. If you don't come around, I'm afraid I will make a bad character witness on your behalf.

Now, don't go taking this to mean I have done anything wrong. I haven't twisted anyone's arm. I haven't even been a whisper in an ear. I don't know what you expect to gain by confronting me. You should mind your own house. I'm watching you.

P.S. This is between you and me.

Strange, huh? But it's a dialogue. He's acknowledged me twice now. Plus, he wants me to keep you out of it. Of course, that makes me want to show you even more. I have to take this to Dr. Muir. I need an expert opinion. You know I could care less about a psychological workup, but I'm not getting anywhere running all about, chasing ghosts. Muir knows his shit. Maybe after I talk with him, something will spark.

I drive into the city. Muir's office is on the 14th floor of the old mercantile building. I don't know how people make this commute every day. To what end are they toiling? They are on a treadmill, and they don't know why. They run and run, never able to pause and consider they're running just to stay in place. Sometimes, I think civilization is shaped only by momentum. People function as they do merely because the ball was already rolling in that direction, and it generated too much force for them to redirect it. Try getting someone to break his schedule. It's like pulling teeth. Try starting a group activity or creating a movement. You're messing with the momentum of life. You're redirecting velocity; that's why they call it a movement. It takes energy—vast amounts of energy—energy I don't have.

Displaced People

The elevator takes me up to the 14th floor and opens to a sterile reception area—modern art with a black and white motif. Spiffy. More so, it reminds me of Mailer—plastic.

"Hi, I'm Hattie Shore. I'm a friend of Dr. Muir. I don't have an appointment, but I have some urgent matters to discuss with him, and I thought I'd just give it a shot." The secretary is staring at me as if I just said all that in Chinese. Maybe she is listening to a phone call. She is wearing one of those Bluetooth earpieces.

"Doctor Muir, there is a Hattie Shore to see you. He just popped in."

I guess she did hear me. I didn't even see her dial, or press a button, or wiggle her nose.

"Um-huh, I'll tell him." She acknowledges me. "The doctor is with someone until three. He says he'll see you after, if you can wait."

I bet she displays just as much personality when she's having an orgasm. For all I know, she is currently having the grand mal of them all.

"What time is it now?" As usual, I hardly pay attention to time.

"2:10," she says, pointing her pen without turning to a digital clock high on the wall behind her.

"I'll wait." So I take a seat in the waiting area. Damn place is nicer than my living room. Because the receptionist's desk is on a platform, the rest of the room feels low. I can't see the woman's lack of expression over the front counter. At least I can see the clock, so I can remain impatient—*watched pot not boiling* and all. Shit, I'm babbling again.

Well, we got some time to kill; what do you want to talk about? Before you ask, I'm not gonna give you a whole bio on me. I wouldn't even tell you half the shit in my head if it weren't for us talking in present tense. That's the great thing about past tense. I can edit my words. Have you ever read Saul Bellow? I can't get through him: pages and pages of thought process. So, if you want to talk, let's make it pertinent—to the point.

I can recommend books ... you want a list? See, there's nothing to talk about. I hate to do this because it feels like cheating, but I can't get my mind off the case to make conversation. So, if you'll excuse my abrasiveness, my lack of cordiality—I'm not much of a host. Best I can think to do is to throw down a little chapter number to help pass the time. Sorry. I got nothing else.

Chapter Two

It's 3:06, and she still hasn't notified me. I've wasted a chapter break on nothing. I got antsy. But what the hell, it's not like chapters are in short supply. If I run out, we can just go to *Part Three* and start all over again, right?

Chapter Three

"Sir, the doctor will see you now." Damn, that took awhile. It's 3:40. I didn't even see anyone leave his office. Was he just catching some Zs? I see into his office as soon as I round the hall's corner. I've never been here before. I always met the doctor on *my* turf. I knew he was high-end, but I had no idea how ritzy. Hanging above his desk, I swear, is a genuine DeKooning. His office looks as if it would make the centerfold for *Better Freuds and Gardens*. I have to wonder how grounded in reality people are who've never been asked if they *want fries with that*.

But, this guy's been spot-on before. He profiled a killer in Boston for me—right on the money. Everything he said was in line with what I read in *Why They Kill*, my bible on psychotic behavior. The author, Richard Rhodes, well defines the moment of epiphany, the instance when the killer says, "To hell with this. All I have to do is discard civilization's rules, and I no longer have to be a victim." They abandon toeing the line and transition from victim to predator. Muir, too, understood it well. I've listened to a lot of shrinks before. They usually remind me of mediums, throwing a ton of darts, hoping one or two will strike center. Muir wasn't like them at all. He said very little. He was pointed and accurate. He will give me a good assessment.

"I was surprised to learn you were here," says Muir.

"Why's that?"

"Didn't think you liked our lot."

"No. That's not the case. I just don't usually worry about motive. It's a can of worms."

"How so?"

"Understanding motive is one step away from excusing action."

"Hm."

I don't want to let him off that easy. "I had this case—this twelve-year-old boy, who had to listen to his mother service her clients in the next room. Once, she was so doped up, she pimped her son out to one guy's friend while she serviced the other in the next room."

"No one should have to go through that," he responded.

"Yeah, only that's not how I met him. I met him when he was arrested for castrating one of his schoolmates. Said they needed to be taught not to be weak."

He grimaces. I like that he doesn't try and sum up my experience in a quaintism. He gestures for me to sit. I do.

"What do you have for me?" he asks.

I slide him the letter. He looks even more the psychotherapist as he dons his reading glasses. Balding, cardigan sweater, tassels on his loafers. Volumes on Picasso and Manet behind him in a glass-enclosed bookshelf. I could easily misjudge him for an affected fool if I didn't know better.

"Do you read those art books much—use the pictures to evaluate your clients?" I joke.

"What? Oh, they've been there since before I lost most of my pretensions." He is still reading.

I'd like to hear about the case where he lost his pretensions. I know he can't or won't tell me. He, too, probably had his moment of epiphany. Perhaps a suicide he should have seen coming. Whatever it was, it knocked him down a notch. Put his feet back on the ground.

He lifts his glasses to his hairline to talk to me. "Well, what do you want—for me to make an assessment based on this limited information?"

"I'm not building a case. I just need to find this guy. Even if you're guessing, this doesn't leave here."

He nods. "What about …?" He motions toward you.

"No, it's cool. The reader's been shadowing me for a while."

"I'm not in the habit of speaking my mind in front of people I don't know."

I'm gonna lie for you, OK? Just play along. "I've asked a friend to read this manuscript to see if it's salable."

"If you say so."

I think you're in. Just keep quiet and read. Don't say anything that will spook him.

"Can I assume there are some misgivings associated with the guy you're after?"

"Yes," I confirm.

"Narcissistic Personality Disorder."

I wait.

"But it's worse than that. He's poking fun at himself, like he knows he's narcissistic."

"He does," I confirm. The doc nods.

"Narcissistic disorders manifest in people who aren't getting the respect they feel they merit, either in the workplace or at home, so they exaggerate or totally fabricate their worth and other's recognition of it. In doing so, they have to downplay the merit of others, which results in a diminishment of empathy. Often, the narcissist is able, but he exaggerates his accomplishments into gestures of near-divine provenance. It is our pleasure just to be in his presence."

The doc is right on the money. I don't need any of this, though. I am not interested in his assessment so much as some ideas, something to break my pattern of *chase, run*.

"This is what really worries me:" he continues, "*I'm watching you.*"

"Yes, but he likes the game. I don't see it as a threat. It's right in line with wanting me to feel his omnipotence," I suggest.

"No. It's not a threat—not now. But, just as he has with others, he could justify harm to you by deciding you brought it on yourself—as if you were the direct mechanism."

"Maybe I can incite him?"

"What do you mean? To come to you?"

The doc leans back in his chair. He respires noisily through his nose. He is out of shape. I wonder about people who seem to breathe laboriously just because they close their mouth. It would scare me.

"You aren't really looking for an assessment; are you?" he asks.

I shrug.

Muir takes another of those nose-wheezing sighs. "I haven't told you anything you don't already know. You're really looking for some ideas on how to incite him. You want to push his buttons so he comes for you. Is that the case?"

"I'm considering that."

"If you challenge his ability, he might want to prove his skills to you on a grand scale, inflicting harm to a great many people. I wouldn't recommend that route."

Again, he's right.

"And if I ignore him?" I ask.

"He'll just find someone else who will be in awe enough to pursue him. He lives for being thought about. He wants you to be obsessed with him. He wants to be the first thing you think about in the morning and the last thing you think about at night."

"He is."

"Well, then you're the right man for his ego. I'm afraid that's all I have for you."

I get up.

"But listen. Be careful with this guy. He'll turn on you and justify it by blaming you. I would take him at his word. He *is* watching you."

"Thanks, doc."

"You two can leave by the back way." He motions to a door across the room. "It leads to the far elevators. This way, my patients don't run into each other in the waiting room. It helps ensure privacy."

That's why I didn't see anyone leave his office earlier. I like simple explanations.

I don't know about your assessment, but I feel caught between a rock and a hard place. I can't challenge or ignore *him*. I'm just gonna have to get creative. Hold on. This may get confusing.

Chapter Four

Harold Finkelstein's life was not what his mother had planned. She wanted him to attend dental school because she knew he wasn't smart enough to be a "real doctor." Harold, however, had no desire to spend his life inside other's mouths, so he went into the porn business. He figured being a big shot porn producer had to increase the likelihood of him getting laid, but so far, all he had accomplished was getting an ex-pro wrestler by the name of John Granite a ton of girls.

Harold had fought John tooth-and-nail over his name change. He'd pleaded with John that Granite was a perfect porn name, but John was obstinate about needing a stage name, so he settled on Marty Poundstone.

It was the third day of shooting for *Watch Your Tuchus, Too*, the second installment of light porn for adventuring middle-aged Jews. The program opened with a justification by a licensed psychiatrist:

"Look, it's not cheating; and who says you're doing anything other than watching a little, right?"

After that, the story began with Marty needing help with his taxes. Into the scene walked this long-legged, stunning blonde with a tight, black miniskirt, dress blouse, and smart, black-rimmed glasses. Jenna was a method actor. She had studied under H&R's assistant vice president in Carlisle in preparation for the role. The assistant vice gnawed through eighty-six pencils during the two weeks she prepared.

Marty recited his line about needing help with large figures. Jenna, knowing Mr. Finkelstein encouraged ad lib, decided to do so even before the love scene. She grabbed the tax form and begun finding legitimate deductions. Marty, not one for adlibbing, raised her skirt, lowered her panties, and mounted her from behind while she continued to spout write-offs. For Finkelstein Productions, it became the most popular tape rental. Stores had to back stock it in preparation for April and June's tax filings.

• • •

"What the hell are you doing?" I ask.

"I thought this would be fun."

"What damn story are we in now? This guy thinks he's Woody Allen."

"It's safe in here," he says. "*This* story will never see the light of day. We can talk in private."

"I don't want to talk. I want to take you in."

He paces the pages. I take a step closer.

"No, stay where you are," he says.

I should keep up the conversation while I try and work my way toward him. If I can just get close enough, I believe I can get a grip on him. "You know I'm not going to stop chasing you."

"I don't get you, *Hattie Shore*. You do realize your name is an anagram, don't you?"

"Yes, I'm well aware of that." I slide my right foot closer and lean forward, edging my left over as he stares off.

"And you don't wonder about that? You aren't curious as to who made you?"

"No, I'm not curious."

"Bull. Do you want to know why you're scared of the dark? You are such a pragmatist, you're afraid if you see a ghost, it won't just frighten you; it will smash down your walls of knowable reality. Your whole belief system will be demolished. One little ghost wrecks everything you stand for."

"I suppose that *is* why I'll never see a real ghost." Closer still.

"Ah, 'real'—I caught that. You said *real*, so if you ever do see an apparition you can write it off as occurring only inside your head."

"You know me too well." Just a little closer.

"When are you going to acknowledge me to the readers? They already know. It's you who is avoiding accepting my nature. I knew you would defy me and show them my letter. Polls say: odds are they're on my side."

"I know. I like being in the minority." I lunge for him. He isn't surprised. Damn jerk was baiting me. He knew all along I was going to make a play for him. Now, where the hell did he go? Over there …

Chapter Five

Two men walk into a bar. The first man says, "I would like to buy a drink for me and my duck."

"We don't serve ducks," says the bartender.

The second man says, "Hey, what the fuck are you doing here? You're messing up the joke."

"It's a stupid joke," I tell him.

"Hence, the name of the book, moron. Now, would you mind moving on?"

"You're really messing up the joke," says the bartender.

"Timing is everything," adds the duck.

"Just tell me where he went," I demand.

"He's with the man from Nantucket."

I jump a few pages, in and out of crappy limericks until I find this one:

> There once was a man from South Brook,
> Who helped hide a man from a book.
> He stuck him in prose

Right under your nose,
Making you look like a schnook.

"Come on. This is getting ridiculous." Nothing. I lost him. I had my chance, and I lost him.

Chapter Six

I lied to him. I never knew my name was an anagram. Damn. Did you figure it out yet? I haven't had a chance to. Maybe you stopped reading when I was in hot pursuit and played with the letters? It's OK. I'm not mad if you left me; I might have done the same thing. Did you get anything? Wait, don't tell me. I'm not listening. Let me decipher it, and we can double-check our answers.

Hattie Shore. That's hoeier. More like a hoe? *Hoeier's* not a word. Guess *that's* is out. *Hates to hire.* What the hell would that mean? *Hate hoister.* No. *Those I heart.* No. *He riots heat?* Probably not. It's about me … me? *Hair to these.* Fuck. Where's my Scrabble?

I pull out the game from my closet. Freaking *H.* I need another *H.* All right. This is better. *Trash,* no. *Hath,* no. *Host the,* no. Damn. There are too many vowels. I need to group more vowels together. *Aerie shot,* no. *Raise the hot,* no. Did it take you this long? Fuck. *Heist the oar,* no. *Atheist …*

Excuse me if I don't get all worked up for figuring it out. Great, so I'm someone's *hero.* How would you feel if you just found out you're not for real? I guess it could be a coincidence, but the pragmatist in me believes Ockham's razor. The others are fictional. All right, so I'm being written too. I suppose I could face that fact. All these years, and I never noticed ... wait, all what years? Who knows when I was written? I suppose you could check the copyright, but maybe I was created well before then in a draft stuffed in a footlocker somewhere. All this time, and I thought I was holding out on you. You knew, didn't you? That's all right. We haven't been entirely honest with each other.

Is it Ara? Did he write me? Probably. Well, fuck him! Did he write that? Fuck Ara! Fuck Ara! Fuck Ara!

What, am I losing my mind? I'm not getting anywhere. This is ridiculous—trying to cope with being *made*. I guess, since I was created, I must have a purpose, right? But why can't I be made and yet not have a purpose? Maybe I was just spit out—*pttooey*—there I am. Are we in different boats? It doesn't stop *you* from going on, unknowing whether or not you were intended. Why should I get so caught up in it? Just because my name is an anagram for *atheist hero*? Is that some sort of proof?

How does the almighty Ara know *he* wasn't made? Maybe he has a purpose? How about that? Huh? This blows. See why I don't get caught up in motives? Speculations go nowhere. This is not my department. I just have to find my man. *I'm watching you.* Are you getting a kick out of this, asshole? I've gotta get my head clear. Maybe a walk around the streets of Manhattan. Nothing like overpopulation to bring things to a boil. The city's like a wedding. The day doesn't bring out the best in brides; it just heightens their already established character. If the bride is a brat, she becomes an extreme tyrant. If she's decent, birds shitting blueberry sauce on her white wedding dress couldn't wreck her day.

I suppose now that I better understand my role in this story—being your narrator—I should set the scene. But, if you remember, I'm not very good with words. Nevertheless, here it goes:

The place looks like a cancer ward. I've traveled back to the '80s, the Reagan era. These are AIDS victims. This guy in the hospital bed likely will be dead by tomorrow. He's too far gone. He probably can't hear us. Sitting in the chair across the way, the man silhouetted by the light coming through the window—it's him. I'd lay money on it.

"Thought you might be here," I venture.

"My little *atheist hero*. How are you?"

"Cut the crap, will you. I didn't go naming myself."

"But you are an atheist?"

"How can I be an atheist when I know you exist?"

"So, you are finally going to acknowledge me in front of the readers?"

"They have no problem making this leap. They're outside the story. They weren't written by Ara."

"You figured that one out too, eh?"

The machines monitoring the dying man's heart bleep at disturbingly long intervals.

"And what about you? Were you created by Ara?" I ask.

"Me? No. I've existed long before Ara."

I nod. I'm not sure if I'm trying to bait him or what. I'm just tired of the search. I continue this only because of that damn smug smile on his face. He thinks he's superior because he's not the whim of some fledgling writer.

I motion toward the hospital bed, the tubes, the machines, the scrap of flesh. "I suppose this guy deserves his lot? After all, he was gay, or a drug user, or had surgery and got transfused with infected blood—you know, *something* deserving of a slow, agonizing extinction."

"I am not responsible for his nor any other's death."

"That's right; you just got the ball rolling. He's the one who brought AIDS on himself. That little girl who was raped and murdered, she shouldn't have worn that sky blue dress, or been out walking alone. Those silly Africans, they shouldn't have been born genetically different. Those Cambodians shouldn't have worn glasses and looked smart. And all those infants shouldn't have attempted to forge out of the womb and expand their lungs to the unwelcoming air. It's their fault, isn't it? It's our fault? We sinned. We are punished."

"It just is."

"If it just is, if bad things happen at random, then what's the sense of prayer? Did the people in Auschwitz not pray as hard as the 2005 Pittsburgh Steelers?"

No answer.

"Either you interfere or you don't. Which is it?"

God is silent.

"Don't give me your rhetorical silence, as if the answer is within me. I *don't* know. Are we flying purely on free will or do you step in on occasion?"

"You are not going to get me to incriminate myself."

"It's only incriminating if you orchestrated this:" I motion to the AIDS victim, then to the walls and beyond.

"It's only incriminating if you step in on occasion to lend support, picking who you help and neglect. It's only incriminating if you aid the tailback in crossing the goal line because he kisses his crucifix and points to the sky, or the pop singer who thanks you for her Grammy before she acknowledges her agent and fans. It's only incriminating if, in the light of all that aid, you ignore those tortured, miserable lives snuffed out in sorrow and anguish, some of them pious to the end."

"They will be at my right hand."

"Couldn't they be at your right hand without the misery? Was their character really so suspect they needed to be tested with evisceration? Is the Hollywood star really so beyond moral reproach, he gets an easier ride into your kingdom? You don't test everyone, now, do you?"

Still silent.

"What did that six-year-old's slaughter teach you about her moral character? But then again, maybe you don't test anyone. Maybe they are all fools to pray because you don't interfere. Maybe you're just one giant note taker. *Honored thy mother and father*—check. *Had no other Gods before me*—check."

"If that's the case, why the hell should we even consider you? There would be no need for prayer. We can just abide by the Commandments and give our thanks to the doctors. Don't worry; we won't assume the surgeons are gods. On occasion, we'll sue them for malpractice just to knock them down a peg. You'll be the only perfect one—setting aside your fault of allowing a world where little girls get raped and killed, of course."

I continue, nearly tripping over my words, trying to spit them out fast enough. "But, I know that's all bunk anyway. You *do* interfere. If you came down in the form of Jesus, or sent him down—whichever—then you interacted with us mortals once again, didn't you? I guess that story and free will don't jibe, do they? Or is it free will after you interfere? Like pushing someone and then seeing if they punch you or not?"

How am I not getting his goat? I thought for sure he would have lunged for me by now.

"I am what I am," he says.

"Yeah, you're about as mysterious as Popeye."

The doctor was right; this narcissist thinks we are so in awe of his presence, even his faults are miraculous. I should leave, but I'm reminded of something else the doc said: This guy would massacre to establish his value. I have to make an attempt at nabbing him so as not to set him off. I must flatter him by showing I'm still interested in his capture.

"Don't bother trying half-heartedly for me," he says, intuitively. "I have nothing to prove to you." He opens the window and the cool evening air rushes in, pulsating the curtain room-dividers. "You may pretend to ignore me, but my presence is everywhere. Goodbye." In two swift moves, he leaps to the sill and out the window. I don't even bother to see if his body is splattered on the sidewalk.

I think I screwed up. I may have talked too much. I don't know what the hell I was thinking. Who says I can hold him even if I do catch him? What am I gonna do, slap the cuffs on him? The man just jumped out a window for Christ's sake.

The thought has occurred to me, though, maybe he doesn't know everything. Maybe, he's just like me, the Corporal, the victims, and in some sense *you*. Not you out there, but the *you* referred to in here. Maybe, he too is the creation of Ara. That would make sense, wouldn't it? After all, why would I be an *atheist hero?* I must be some sort of personification of Ara's own struggle over the intellectual necessity for God. And, if that's the case, Ara may have personified God, as well, to make his argument. There's really only one way to find out. I *have* to slap the cuffs on God. If I can hold him, he's not the real McCoy, but a character like the rest of us. That would leave room for there not really being a God. That would leave room for the legitimacy of atheism. The best I can do is to put my faith in the creativity of man.

Chapter Seven

Did you see the news this morning? A religious cult committed mass suicide in Iowa. Their dictum was *Embrace God*. Am I supposed to take this seriously? God's mocking my inability to nab him while simultaneously punishing me for questioning his importance. What's the sense of caring? I'm like Sisyphus, tasked with an unattainable objective. I can't catch God, and when I mess up, people die. Worst of all, none of them even exist to begin with. I'm tearing myself up over fictitious atrocities, phony causes, and fake lives.

I can't get over that I'm a character, a notion, existing only on paper and in other's minds. The meaninglessness of my life was fine with me as long as it was on my terms. Now that I know my life is predetermined, I no longer wanna play. I don't appreciate being used as a pawn for someone else's musings. I wouldn't respect myself if I continued along this path—with this chase.

I don't care how much God baits me. I am not giving credence to him, Ara, nor anyone or anything else in this made-up world. In fact, I am going to do whatever I can to throw a wrench in it all.

The barrel of my pistol is warmer than I expected inside my mouth.

I had awaited the sensation of *cold steel*, but my body heat warmed the barrel as it lay in my side holster. I rotate myself, back to the wall, so as not to make a mess on my new couch. I wonder if other suicides were concerned with the trajectory of their brain matter. Who should really care, right? In a moment, I'll have none. To my back is the brick wall of the tenement. I don't want an errant shot to ricochet through the floor above and harm a neighbor. But really, why should that matter? They are just like me—created for the world of print. Unless I shoot them, they may not even get ink in this book. Come to think of it, their best chance at existence is if I involve them in my exploits. No, I know better than to think I have any control; and I'm beyond being one's puppet.

"What are you doing?"

It's him.

"I'm not mad. I just thought you may have lost faith in me," he says.

I pull the barrel out of my mouth. "God ... whoever, do whatever you want. I'm through."

"Are you trying to present me with some sort of ethical dilemma? You know it is a sin to kill yourself, but you also know it is against my doctrine of free will to try and convince you not to."

My eyes are a blank. I am not processing this. He senses my hopelessness. In his expression is the need for recognition, almost a plea. He realizes I am not absorbing his words. I usually analyze every movement, yet now, I have no interest in the riddle before me.

I put the barrel back into my mouth and think only about the angle of trajectory. Even in this fictitious life, I still feel obligated not to harm others. I thumb off the safety, almost sensing the red ring around the neck of the button. The trigger is awkward to pull when the gun faces me. I never fired my gun with my wrist bent like this. It would normally mean bad marksmanship.

"WAIT!" he yells.

I ease the trigger back, hovering the hammer over the pin.

"I'm not interfering, but wait!" He advances on me.

The next sound is like a symphony to my heart—the metallic tone I've been dreaming of ever since my creation.

Clink, zip. The handcuff wraps around God's arm; the other bracelet already secure on my own left wrist, hidden under my baggy shirt sleeve. I ease the hammer back by releasing the tension on the trigger, and I remove the barrel from my mouth.

God stares down at his shackled wrist. "But I'm omniscient. How did I not see that coming?"

"All I had to do was not narrate my actions to the reader, and you wouldn't be privy to my plan. You need me to pursue you. Without my searching for you, what kind of existence do you have?"

Everything I previously said in this chapter has been a big lie. I've had one ambition: to capture him. My suicide was all a ruse. I slept for days with the handcuffs on my own wrist. I never spoke or even thought about what I was doing. I knew, as he said, he was watching me. That's what gave me the idea. I had to lure him to me instead of continuing my futile chase. I had faith in man all along. Ara wouldn't have created me, the conflict, in vain. He has some point. It's man who is the creator, man who invents the reason for being. Man decides and establishes his character.

"So, now what?" God asks.

"Now I take you in."

"On what charge? I haven't done anything."

"Don't you watch your *Law and Order*? You set a course of action foreseeably leading to the harm of others. The charge is *reckless endangerment*."

"Who's going to judge *Me*?"

"I suppose a jury of your peers."

PART THREE

Chapter One

Marcus climbed the dull grey courthouse stairs while thumbing through his attaché case to ensure, for the third time in ten minutes, he had all his paperwork. He reached the top steps, plopped his case onto the ground and rifled through it looking for his small yellow steno pad while simultaneously minding his contents from being caught in the wind eddy formed by the clash of the air stream and the large concrete structure.

"I'm a fucking mess," he muttered.

Twenty minutes later, he stood in front of the judge, representing the great city of New York as an assistant district attorney. The courtroom hummed with small-talk between onlookers, lawyers, defendants, and family members—all packed inside the pew-and-spindle laden interior. The volume rose until the judge banged his gavel and gained control of the crowd, only to hear the conversational buildup begin anew. Marcus barely looked up from his notes to address the robed figure. He spoke in a light drone, as if giving his words a cursory run through.

"Your Honor, we request the defendant be remanded into custody ..."

"Your Honor!" interjected the highly dramatic Chuck Laughton with phony southern charm devised in lieu of his upbringing in the

Connecticut suburbs. "My client is not being charged with murder, but rather the lesser crime of reckless endangerment. We feel bail is not only in order, but perhaps a requisite for such an offense."

Marcus, half-startled by the foreseeable objection, with effort, spoke more vigorously, at a sudden polarity from his earlier composure. "Your Honor, though the defendant is being charged with the lesser crime of reckless endangerment, there are more than ten million counts before him in this state alone; and we are still compiling histories. Yes, withholding bail has little precedent on such a charge, but the magnitude and consistency of the offenses establishes the defendant's inability to curb his felonious activities." Marcus lowered his papers, a tactic he had developed to suggest what follows comes straight from the heart. "Not to mention, Your Honor, that the defendant can arrange for any amount of capital desired, and that we deem him a substantial flight risk, with or without a passport."

"Thank you for not mentioning it," said Judge O'Hare, who deemed himself a wit.

"Your Honor," sang Laughton. "Are we to assume there will be no more deaths while my client is in custody."

"I'm not following your point," replied the judge.

Laughton continued Socratically, as if he were exposing a particularly insightful passage to a bunch of freshmen philosophy students. "What's the point of remanding my client if deaths will continue to ensue with him in custody? Is the state going to charge him with the events unfolding at present and in the future though he is detained? If they are, then why shouldn't he be given leave on his own recognizance? Again, he is not being charged with murder, and the course of events is already in motion."

"Your Honor," interjected Marcus, "that argument holds about as much water as releasing a defendant on the grounds that his hospitalized victim is likely to die from his injuries, with or without the defendant in custody. It is irrelevant. Again, I remind the court of the defendant's penchant for vanishing and the immensity of the search just to apprehend him in the first place. Your Honor, if we …"

"The defendant is a pillar of the community—an avatar of moral righteousness," interrupted Laughton.

"You have to be kidding me; there are forty-nine other states waiting to prosecute him."

Judge O'Hare repeatedly struck his gavel to stop the bickering. "Gentlemen, we are not trying the case now. The defendant will be held without bail. District date set for …" he paused while the assistant pointed to dates in the judge's open calendar. "May 16th. That's all."

Laughton waited for Marcus in the courthouse atrium. Instinctively, Marcus desired to avoid his opponent, more because he tired of the man's rhetoric than felt him a professional threat.

"What now?" Marcus asked, exhaustedly dragging his feet across the black-and-white checkered marble way.

"No jury, no trial," Laughton replied, extending a brief with his customary smug certainty.

Marcus stubbornly avoided accepting the document. "Aren't you a little premature in filing a motion? I haven't even made my prima facie."

"I'd like to establish, early on, the futility of this whole prosecution."

Marcus grabbed the motion and inquired as to its contents, unwilling to open and read it in front of Laughton, thus not giving him the satisfaction of seeing Marcus wince. "Are you asking for a change of venue?" he probed, waving the brief.

"No, I'm not concerned with people having heard about the case. In fact, I think my client's notoriety is to my advantage." Laughton shifted his papers from his right side to his left. "I don't see how you can expect twelve ordinary mortals to pass judgment on *Him*."

"So, what then? You want a trial by judge?"

Laughton chuckled. "You know the personal histories of these judges as well as I do. No, we are not going to have another crucifixion with one central figure washing his hands of it all and blaming the noncorporal law. This case never gets started. Marcus, you are so over your head, you don't even know."

Marcus suppressed his response. He didn't want to show any more of his hand than necessary. Too much fishing would be read as weakness.

Fortunately for Marcus, he was able to stay the motion hearing until after the prima facie. Judge Silvia Hendershot acknowledged the absurdity of addressing motions prior to establishing a credible case. And since she would not be presiding beyond the establishment of the prima facie, she saw no need to become overly involved. Let the assigned judge address motions.

Laughton was unfazed. His prime tactic was to throw wrenches into the system's works, knowing it was not *his* time devoted to sorting through the havoc. Most of his motions were denied, but their real damage was in the consumption of the prosecutor's time and the instigated desire by judges to augment settlements and plea agreements. He hoped most people just wanted him to go away.

Judge Hendershot found sufficient grounds for trial, mainly because Laughton did not put up much evidence contrary to the charge. He didn't want the prosecution to get a preview of the trial, if the case were to make it that far. Laughton preferred to attack via motions, testing the credibility of the system. To initially put up a defense would be to acknowledge the right of the court to try his client. He was not yet prepared for such acquiescence. As a last resort, if the case ever did go to trial, Laughton had to win over only one juror. He had no reason to show his hand prematurely and allow Marcus time to polish his rebuttal.

Judge Hendershot, knowing the case would not fall to her, recognized sufficient grounds to adjudicate the actions of the defendant. In fact, God was already being judged by the public. The topic was addressed in arenas involving common discourse to formal university lectures, from Jung to Mencken. In addition, several books were written on the subject, including: *Where Is God When It Hurts?* and *Why Do Bad Things Happen to Good People?* Marcus had even mentioned trials held in absentia in concentration camps. Most people who fancied themselves intellectuals desired the trial as long as they could distance themselves from the outcome and avoid expressing any definitive opinion. For Judge Hendershot to find legal merit was more noncommittal than squashing the case outright. A dismissal would find God blameless. Declaring merit simply deferred responsibility.

After the formal arraignment, the rotation fell to Judge Ishiguru who set the date for the pretrial conference, during which time he would address the premature motion and set a date for conclusion of future motions and trial if it got that far. Inside Ishiguru's chambers, Laughton presented his objection.

"Your Honor, a jury of his peers? Come on."

Marcus dove right in. "So, if we are to have a member of the elite in any field stand trial are we to assume no ordinary citizen is fit to pass judgment? We try professionals whose motives incorporate complex technical analyses. We present evidence which it took highly trained specialists to develop. It is not the counsel's place to decide which information is too complex for me to present."

"He does have a point," said Ishiguru, his sandaled feet propped up on the ottoman he kept by his leather and mahogany desk. His right hand rested lazily on his stomach while his left rotated the grip end of a putter, pirouetting on his Afghani area rug. The two lawyers loomed ominously over his desk, their importance ironically mitigated by the seated and diminutive judge. To Ishiguru, every discussion had an academic air removed from the gravity of any repercussions resulting from his ultimate decisions. The judge continued. "After all, the onus is on Marcus to present the evidence in a manner that can be understood at trial."

Laughton fired back. "But that's just the point, Your Honor. We are talking about mechanisms beyond human comprehension. We are talking about *mysterious ways*. No juror is qualified to even attempt to comprehend the motives, actions, and reactions of my client. They too would have to be omniscient."

"What about you?" replied Marcus. "Are you omniscient? Are you able to understand his case? If not, I suppose you will return your fee and walk away from representing the biggest client of your career?"

Ishiguru smirked.

"Your Honor," sang Laughton, as he spread his arms in a sacrificial pose. Marcus recognized the sing-song response of Laughton when cornered. "Am I to deny a client counsel? I don't pretend to understand the absolute inner workings of my client's mind."

"Nor would you or a jury have to personally relate to the inner workings of the mind of a schizophrenic, a serial killer, or anyone mentally disturbed," Marcus added.

"Game, set, and match," said Ishiguru. He swung his legs off the ottoman and leaned forward, this time hugging the putter, the grip running along the side of his cheek. "We go to trial; set your calendars for March." Ishiguru looked up from his appointment book to address Laughton. "And I'm warning you ahead of time, if you make a mockery out of my voir dire, there will be hell to pay."

Laughton knew it was an empty threat. Of course, he had plans for voir dire—the equivocation of the term *peers* aside.

"Agreed," said Laughton.

Ishiguru stared a moment at Laughton and considered one more preemptive warning. "And I don't want to hear a word about incompetent representation. Your check cleared; you're competent. You got me, counselor?"

"Yes, sir."

Outside the judge's chambers, Marcus openly gloated. "Guess it's set," he said, feeling Laughton out—knowing there was another shoe to drop.

"Nice try," said Laughton. "You know better. That was just baby stuff. Warm-up strokes. Mark my words, this ship don't sail." He handed Marcus another motion.

"I thought it was 'that dog don't hunt'?"

"You get the idea." He jabbed Marcus paternally on the shoulder and strode away. Laughton always strode away as if his day was *just made*. But, earlier in chambers, Marcus had heard him sing his futile plea: "Your Honor," with his arms dangling in the air, as if in need of a hug. He wanted to keep Laughton singing.

Chapter Two

"It's brilliant."

Maria Anna Stephanopolous. Hot. She was built for fetishism—authoritatively sultry and with glasses. Her mix of jet black hair, professional competence, and tight skirts was like a Betty Page tribute. When she was assigned a city position, lawyers, paralegals, even mail clerks thought maybe someone was paying attention to their midnight prayers. Marcus called her into his office, relying on his typical, rather banal, sense of humor.

"Mary, Ann, Steph—all three of you—could you come in here, please?" He knew he could only use the corny jibe possibly one more time before it got tired. Fortunately, she was still new enough to appreciate his attempt, even if she was merely suffering the joke. He couldn't help but to analyze her smile as she entered. Marcus uncertainly read her manner and decided it was best to assume she was just being nice and he should retire the jest. He would have to hit upon some other PC way of feigning humor. It was Marcus' bane in life to find common discourse more trying than the elaborate wordings of a lawyer's communiqué.

He watched her read the brief, noting her slow head shakes, a sign of esteem for the opposition. He became conscious of watching her, again sending out PC warning flares. *Could it be construed ogling? It wasn't like she was chewing on the tip of her pen.*

Damn it. He was getting a hard-on. He knew it was more from lack of sleep than anything else. She lowered the document.

"It's brilliant. He's brilliant."

Marcus disliked having a serious discussion while aroused. He worried it spoke ill of his professional commitment. He would continue as normal, knowing the table hid his excitement and hope the erection would subside once he could get his mind off it. He tried further analyzing his shame to divert his thoughts from his arousal. Perhaps, the guilt was a byproduct of finding fault with a part of his body not dedicated to the trial; as if his boner should know better than to rear its head at such a serious time.

"What are you thinking about?" Maria asked.

"I'm thinking about this raging hard-on in my pants." *Did he just say that out loud?* Marcus stared wide-eyed at Maria.

His world stopped.

Maria smirked, then made a series of movements Marcus had seen before only on the Playboy channel, though he had read about such things in *Forum*. In one fluent motion, she undid her hair braid, snatched off her glasses, and shook her jet black mane down around her shoulders.

"Funny, because all this attention to briefs has me horny," she said, spying the bulge in his pants.

"Well, I have the cure for that," he uncharacteristically said.

Maria swooped down and planted a long passionate kiss on him. "We are sooo bad for doing this instead of working on our case," she cooed.

"I know. At this pace, we'll never get anything done and ..." Those troublesome words broke Marcus from his dialogue, and he pushed Maria away from him. "Wait. This is wrong."

"I don't mind," she replied through a sexy pout.

"No, not like that. I mean, this isn't really supposed to happen."

"It's strange you say that, because I don't remember being all that attracted to you in the past," said Maria, arranging her already disheveled tresses.

Marcus sprang to his feet, slapped his palm onto the phone's handset, dialed, and huffed into the receiver, "Where is he?"

"Behind bars. Where do you think?" replied the prison assistant administrator, knowing it was Marcus.

"No, I mean *where is he, right now?*"

"You want his schedule? That I don't have."

"Find him. Secure him. Put him in lockdown," ordered Marcus.

"I can't just do that. Besides, no offense, Marcus, but I don't work for you. We speak as a courtesy. What you want is over my head."

"Then get me the warden."

The lackey huffed into the phone—a display of the enormous physical effort needed to rouse the warden. Marcus ignored the histrionics.

"All right. Hold on." There was a pause for nearly a minute, after which, the receiver was fumbled on the other end. "He's in a meeting."

"Interrupt."

"It's the kind of meeting I shouldn't interrupt."

"Look, I know he is balling his secretary or whomever. Now, you get his attention, and get him on the phone, RIGHT FUCKING NOW!"

"OK … chill." Another long pause. The receiver was fumbled again.

"This better be good," demanded the warden.

"Where is he right now?"

"If he's like the others, he's watching *Springer* right now. Why?"

"No wonder. He's getting ideas. Lock him down, now!"

"Is there a threat?"

"If you don't want me to tell the Mrs. about your little tryst, you'll lock him down now."

There was another long pause. Marcus was about to speak when the warden broke the silence first. "All right."

Marcus hung up the phone. His erection was gone. "I can't believe this. He's trying to derail us."

"What do you mean?" asked Maria.

"That was uncharacteristic of you and certainly uncharacteristic of me," said Marcus.

"Why is the emphatic associated with *your* uncharacteristic act? Are you insinuating I shtupp my coworkers?"

"No, no … that's not it," he stammered. "I just mean, *I can only assume about you.* I know about me."

"What the hell does that mean?"

Marcus saw the grave getting deeper. "Look, I don't know what the hell I'm saying. Let's not replace sex with fighting. It's all unproductive. Can we just get back to the case? I have to present in three days, and as you said, this one's a doozey."

Maria weighed throwing the table at him versus dropping the incident altogether. She looked down at the brief then returned her attention to Marcus, opting to reapply herself to legal concerns. "Well, there's no doubt it's brilliant. He's testing the system in ways unlike anyone I've ever seen or heard about."

Marcus exhaled in relief.

"I must admit, I'm unsure where to begin with this one," he said. "Laughton has long established he isn't afraid to challenge the system. And in this case, he may be on to something."

"How do we respond?"

Marcus stared at the brief, thinking.

Chapter Three

"Your Honor," began Laughton, "it's really quite simple. My client is charged with creating circumstances that wantonly led to the harm of others. He is accused of manipulating the natural course of actions."

Laughton shifted in the plush leather chair, crossed his legs, and continued with the certainty of the uninterruptable.

"Our whole legal system is based upon the concept of free will. The law assumes we have the ability to control our behavior, adjust our actions and reactions, so when we act egregiously, we are to be held responsible for our behavior. Only those deemed incapable of understanding right verses wrong or those experiencing diminished control are able to mitigate and sometimes avoid legal repercussions.

"Now, if we are to assume, as the courts must for them to dole out punishment, that people are generally accountable for their own behavior, then we've refuted the charge before us. My client is not responsible for man's atrocities, but man himself is responsible, and the charges must be dropped, as free will exonerates him.

"But, if we are to assume free will doesn't exist—if we are to assume man can't deviate from the course of action set in motion by my client, then the court system has no grounds to hold *anyone* accountable for their actions, as all actions are predetermined, including those actions of my client, for the law can't have one specific set of rules that apply only to him.

"In short, Your Honor, if there is free will, my client is not responsible for what befell the victims. If there is no free will and events and actions are determined, then how can the court punish those for acts beyond their control?"

Laughton stopped as abruptly as he began, finishing his speech with a flourishing raise of the eyebrows, as if to insinuate what he had just said was self-evident.

During this didactic speech, Ishiguru sat attentively quiet. This was the first motion on his docket for the day. Ishiguru considered making it the last one, but he knew his patience would wear thin near workday's end. Besides, the need to keep schedule would ensure the speed of the hearing—the two attorneys knowing they didn't have the evening to eat into. Normally, Ishiguru lounged during the discussion of motions, but today, he sat forward and upright with his hands on his desk. He had placed the opposing lawyers across from him and told them, rather than to *keep it brief*, to present their position in full, so there would not be constant rebutting. In turn, he would interrupt seldom, if at all, hoping the lawyers would exhaust themselves without the invigorating infusion of probing questions.

When Laughton finished, Ishiguru let out a long sigh. He was either annoyed by the insinuation of the court's impotency or impressed by the strength of the rhetoric. Either way, Ishiguru forcibly suppressed his usual need to question.

"Well, what of it, counselor?" He gestured to Marcus, trying to display weariness so the rebuttal would be brief. Marcus was stymied by the judge's lack of academic enthusiasm. He never before witnessed Ishiguru so taciturn. He read the silence as a poor omen for himself; perhaps Laughton's volley of activity was having its desired effect. Marcus began slowly, as if checking an iced lake for sturdiness.

"Well, Your Honor, on the face of it, Laughton's argument seems air tight in its *Catch-22* logic. He presents us with a syllogism: either free will implicates man and exonerates God or determinism takes away the court's footing to mete out blame.

"It's all fine and dandy until you take into account that the syllogism is false. There are alternatives. Suppose all is determined except for the actions of the accused. Suppose he had the choice of creating a material, deterministic world. If he did, then he is equally responsible for the end consequences. His guilt is the result of one action, the first cause, which spiraled out the injurious circumstances."

"Slippery slope. Slippery slope, Your Honor," butted in Laughton.

Ishiguro shot him a glance suggesting *I will have none of that.* Laughton closed his gaping mouth and leaned back into his chair.

Marcus continued. "Take for example the double Y aggression chromosome defense. The buck doesn't stop with the YY if the defendant is the one who created the YY in the first place."

"Am I to infer Hostess should be held responsible in the Twinkie defense," interjected Ishiguro.

"Not unless Hostess could reasonably foresee their actions would directly precipitate the circumstances resulting in an injury. It is the very nature of the defendant's omniscience that damns him. He is the creator of the determining factors, therefore he should be held responsible for all ensuing results. It makes no difference that he is not pulling the strings day to day.

"Conversely, if we consider the free-will defense, we can find gray areas there as well. Perhaps man has free will, with God's interjection on occasion, as describe in Holy Scripture. God's act would taint the purity of free will, much as a scientist can skew the outcome of an experiment with his presence, or the way reality TV is influenced by the presence of the camera. Determining such a degree of interaction is exactly what a trial is for. It is my job to establish the accused's culpability during trial. It would be premature to assume his noncomplicity prior to New York's right to present its case. Even with the extreme example of the defendant granting man free will, I would still have the right to establish he knowingly foresaw the consequences of said free will.

"Your Honor, whether the accused created havoc day to day or by one egregious event is not of relevance. All that matters is that, but for his actions, atrocities would not have occurred."

Marcus took a huge breath, slowly exhaled, and observed the judge digesting his remarks. "Your Honor, I have assembled the key points for your review at a later time," he remarked.

Ishiguru held up his hand, staving off the notes. "No need. I will decide on this matter now."

Laughton and Marcus shot glances at each other. Neither had expected the judge to make a ruling on the motion without review. Laughton thought for sure he would have a chance to make Marcus sweat, perhaps even get the offer of a plea bargain. Marcus hoped he could at least have a day or two to tell his colleagues *things looked promising* or *all went well. But who was he kidding?* Privately, he wasn't even sure if the courts of New York should have jurisdiction over the actions of the Creator.

Chapter Four

Tom, the red-haired clerk, walked past the seven-foot, coin-operated pool table. He carried a cocktail tray with shots of Jager to the table at the farthest end of the room. "How in the hell can Ishi justify trying God?" asked Lewin, Esq.

"How can *I* justify it?" retorted Marcus, puffing a plume of cigar smoke into the already smog-thick air.

"Well, it's not like you have a choice. You take the cases as they come," said Morton, Esq.

"Great. Ishi can avoid hubris by neutrally deferring judgment to twelve jurors. I can by claiming duty. The jurors ... well, that's the real question. They too are in their position by force of obligation; but that doesn't mean they will convict. I'd hate to be them. They have no choice but to decide God's fate. Can you imagine the pressure of that decision? If I were truly noble, I would settle and spare those folks the weight of that judgment. Only, Laughton would never agree to reasonable terms."

"I'm just amazed you got this far," said Lewin, Esq.

Marcus nodded in somber agreement. The collective of lawyers and the red-haired clerk huddled around the man of the hour.

"Why didn't you argue trying God was a determined result of his first actions," offered Morton, Esq.

"Or that we have the free will to try him," threw in Lewin, Esq. Neither lawyer waited for an answer from Marcus.

Marcus expected them to *Monday morning quarterback* the motion hearing, and he knew they would go down the wrong path. Suggesting Ishiguru's degree of control was grander than those of the accused would make the judge gun-shy.

"Hey, good job," said Lewin, Esq. and raised his shot.

"To one small step," said Marcus.

"For man," replied Tom. Marcus hesitated, taking in full Tom's rider.

"For man," said Marcus.

"For man," said the two other lawyers, and all four downed their shots.

Lewin, Esq. nearly choked his shot back up, holding the glass away from his bent over body, dripping brown fluid onto the already liquor-stained floor boards. "What the fuck was that?" he asked.

"Jager," replied Tom. "Why, what did you think it was?"

"Blackberry brandy."

"That's a girly drink," laughed Tom. "Welcome to the big leagues."

"Oh yeah?" said Lewin, Esq. feeling challenged. "Come with me. We're doing an Irish Car Bomb." Lewin, Esq. and Tom shoved each other over to the bar.

"Nepotism is a beautiful thing," said Morton, Esq., watching uncle and nephew let loose. Marcus sat and mindfully stabbed out his cigar. Morton, Esq. joined him at the table.

"So, what did the samurai have to say?" asked Morton, Esq.

Marcus swirled a quarter-filled glass of warm beer. "He actually admonished Laughton for suggesting the impotency of the court system. He flat out said a ruling in his favor would establish precedent for every child molester on down to claim they are an unswerving consequence of their historical makeup, hence, unable to do other than the crimes they committed. It would be the undoing of our legal system. He ruled then

Displaced People

and there in favor of free will. Never thought I'd see the day the courts would settle a scientific conundrum. Next thing they'll do is rule light is a photon and never a wave."

Marcus held up his beer in a mock toast. "There you have it, the courts of New York have solemnly declared: *There is no such thing as determinism. Spinoza is spinning in his grave.*"

Marcus lowered his glass without finishing off its contents. "We're all full of shit."

"Yes we are," agreed Morton, Esq. and clinked his glass against Marcus' abandoned drink, as if it were a new toast.

. . .

The following morning, Maria entered Marcus' office carrying a brief like a hot potato. She extended the papers to the seated Marcus and waited with her free hand on her hip. Marcus looked up from his computer, only to be crushed by having to engage, yet again, another philosophical mind game.

"Now what," he asked disheartened.

"He's asking for the judge to recuse himself."

Shocked, Marcus asked, "On what grounds?"

"Bias. The judge has a parent who died of Alzheimer's and an uncle who was shot to death in a grocery store holdup."

Marcus reluctantly read the brief. "Laughton says the judge is predisposed to blaming his client for creating an environment where his own loved ones were subject to harm." He lowered the brief. "I don't believe this. Are we ever going to address real legal issues? How long do we have?"

"To reply?"

"No, 'til the motion deadline?"

"March 1st."

"I hope we survive."

Maria leaned against the door jamb. "If he wins this motion, there

131

won't be a single judge, juror, or prosecutor deemed *without a bone to pick with God*. If Ishi is biased, who isn't?"

Marcus dropped his forehead onto his forearm and rocked the tension around his skull. He spoke into his lap. "Get me a professor." He looked up at Maria through bloodshot eyes. "Get me a Harvard or MIT brain who can refute this crap. I'm tired. I can't think along these lines. Get me someone who can."

Maria nodded and walked out of the office with a purposeful stride.

• • •

Judge Ishiguru slammed the brief onto his desk.

"Calm down, Ishi," soothed Judge Pierce.

"This is an outrage," Ishiguru said sternly.

"There is a modicum of truth to it, don't you think?"

"No. I won't be told I'm biased. I'm the perfect judge for this. I'm a Buddhist."

"What would that matter?" inquired Pierce.

"I don't know. I don't know what I'm saying," said Ishiguru, throwing up his arms in exasperation.

"Maybe you're looking a gift horse in the mouth. Here's your out. Recuse yourself, and you can avoid going down as Pontius Pilate II."

"That damn Laughton," grunted Ishiguru.

• • •

Laughton slammed his briefcase onto the metal tabletop of the visitor's room.

"This is an outrage. The judge isn't even going to address the motion. Ishi claims it is the equivalent of asking a judge to recuse himself because he lives in the city a defendant may end up residing in. If that were the case, he said, every judge would have to be imported from out of state. It would cause legal gridlock."

"He's right," said God.

"Of course he's right. But he stopped Marcus from having to spend time and resources addressing our motion. He killed two to three good days of sabotage—that smug Solomon." Laughton sat down across from his client, slightly embarrassed by his exaggerated display of anger. He recognized the absurdity of fabricating ire for his omniscient client, but the visit established billable activity. He hoped to look busy enough in front of the guards, prison administrators, and colleagues to justify his fee. The more logs he could sign, the better.

Laughton searched for something to discuss with his client, but he rarely delved into the personal arena, mainly because he could never remember if he already inquired about his client's status. *Single? Married? Kids? Names? Ages? Gender? Location?* If he already supposedly knew about such things, his *forgetfulness* would reveal his true level of interest. Laughton befriended many people, soon acting too familiarly to re-inquire about their names. Frequently, he referred to acquaintances as *captain*, to cover his tracks.

He gazed across the sturdy table into the black holes of his client's eyes, afraid of looking too deeply and crossing the event horizon of God's perception. Laughton flinched and fiddled with his briefcase. His client's calm unnerved him. "Are you even paying attention?"

"Yes. I'm doing two things at once."

"What else are you doing?"

• • •

Marcus dropped his pants and fondled the buttocks of Tom the red-headed clerk, nephew of Lewin, Esq.

"This is so uncharacteristic of me," said Tom.

"At this rate, I'll never get any work done," added Marcus.

"Are you even gay?" asked Tom.

"No, why? Are you?"

Chapter Five

Two hundred fifty potential jurors were summoned for duty. The judge wanted a wide selection to stave off all possible delay by the defense. Ishiguru did not foresee the time that would be consumed by the prosecutor's objections.

Marcus and Laughton remained seated at their respective long wooden tables, too vast an area for the few piles of papers before them—a collection of jury names, their corresponding numbers, individual questionnaires, and loose-leaf for notes.

Laughton never considered hiring a professional consultant for voir dire. In fact, jury selection was his favorite part of the trial. He felt like a coach putting together a fantasy football team. Laughton believed the trial was won or lost right here. *Who cares if you present an ironclad defense if it falls on deaf ears? Better to mount a superficial defense to a patently sympathetic jury.* Besides, Laughton felt the odds were in his favor, not just for this particular case, but in general.

Winning trials was like quitting smoking—it took only one relapse to fail. To successfully quit, one must die never having smoked again. Then, friends and family at the wake can say, "Well, I guess he quit for good."

With trials, the prosecution had the burden of winning over each and every person, the equivalent of never smoking again; but the defense need convince only one person to light up.

Fueled by the drive to pick a winning jury—to pick one bad apple or good apple depending on the perspective—Laughton studied every known text on the subject of *reading people,* to include the *Facial Action Coding System* Manual. He even digested books on poker to learn the various *tells* displayed in the game.

Laughton understood that no set interpretation of mannerisms or tells existed—every gesture and response had to be considered in its context. For example: a person with his arms crossed can be emotionally defensive, physically cold, or both; or something else entirely. Still, Laughton felt leagues beyond his adversaries, as they pursued the fine letter of the law instead of the gamesmanship. And his uncanny successes validated his approach. He wasted the defense's time and resources, infuriating all involved—including the judge.

Laughton relied on man's propensity toward stasis, even if declining action meant accepting inferiority. Most people preferred to be rid of strife more than they desired exacting conclusions. Laughton acknowledged human fatigue. The other lawyers practiced as if computers were going to respond to all motions and decisions—void of tiring, void of emotions, void of history. But judges tired, lawyers tired, even the public tired. Eventually, everyone just wanted Laughton to go away, and they often acquiesced without going to trial. Let his adversaries spend precious time attempting to be faultless with the law. Laughton never let scattershot error slow his bombardment. He practiced blitzkrieg law while his adversaries performed time-consuming, effortful, precision strikes.

And, Laughton's clincher was his ability to pick a sympathetic jury— to somehow poison the pool. Ultimately, if need be, Laughton could always fall back on the idea of law. He *could*, if pressured, present a hell of a defense, and win on merit of position alone. But that would be a last-ditch tactic.

The prosecution, on the other hand, lacked the funds for anything like a voir dire consultant. Besides, the New York office always hired top-of-their-class applicants, too proud to acknowledge the human penchant for the illogical in trial law. For people like Marcus, voir dire was to ensure no preconceptions crept into the jury box, as opposed to Laughton, who banked on those preconceptions.

Ishiguru realized the blunder in his own expectations on the very first of Marcus' challenge for cause. The judge had warned Laughton about obfuscations with the term *peers* and whatever other tricks he had up his sleeve, but Ishiguru didn't realize the best trick Laughton had was to simply give Marcus enough rope to hang himself.

Laughton opened the door by asking the first man—number eighty-four—his religious beliefs.

"I'm a Christian," the man replied. Laughton nodded and sat, gesturing to the man for Marcus to proceed.

Marcus recklessly took the defense's bait.

"And as a Christian, do you have any problem with being able to find God guilty if the evidence should establish such—of passing judgment on *Him?*"

The man's eyes widened, and he shifted nervously in his chair. "Oh, I don't think I could do that," he said. "No, I'm not the right guy to judge God."

Marcus turned to Ishiguru and made his first *challenge for cause* on the grounds the potential juror could not "weigh the evidence fairly and objectively."

Laughton let out a small "ack," sounding his contempt, but no more. Ishiguru acknowledged the challenge and dismissed the first juror.

When the following seven jurors voiced similar lack of confidence at being able to objectively judge the defendant, Laughton made his move.

"Your Honor, counsel for the prosecution is wasting our time. If the prosecution is waiting for a jury of atheists, may I remind Your Honor of the statistics? Nonbelievers make up only four percent of the population. To get twelve jurors, we would have to interview three hundred people without my peremptory challenges. After I challenge the first ten due to philosophical bias, which is well within my right, it would take another two hundred fifty, making a total of five hundred fifty interviews, providing we don't hit a nonbeliever dry-spell. It would take another hundred and fifty to get the four alternates as I have two more strikes there as well. That would take months and months, perhaps nearly a year, an unfair burden for my client, assured a speedy trial."

Ishiguru sucked in a vast amount of air and huffed out his dismay over agreeing with Laughton. "Well, what of it, counselor?" the judge asked Marcus. "Any chance you'll relax your criteria?"

"Not really, Your Honor," Marcus replied. "Batson does not extend to religious affiliation, and the potential jurors all disqualified themselves due to their acknowledged bias."

Laughton pounced on Marcus' staunch stance. "Your Honor, being as most minority groups are involved in religious communities, I suspect these challenges are a pretext for racial discrimination, whether intentional or not."

Ishiguru now saw Laughton's plan for what it was—the engineering of a mistrial. And it was too late; Laughton had made his objection part of the record. If there ever was going to be a valid trial, Ishiguru had to get Marcus to flex.

"I'm inclined to agree with the defense that your blanket challenges are excessive, and I will not allow this process to be delayed, wasting the tax-payers' money. You are going to have to start accepting jurors."

"What would Your Honor have me do?" asked Marcus. "Allow the empanelling a jury of people unwilling to find the defendant guilty regardless of my case?"

"Maybe you need to make a distinction between *unwilling* and *reluctant*," said the judge, finding his own words grating.

"But, Your Honor …"

Ishiguru held up his hand, interrupting the objection so he could continue.

"You knew the unpopularity of this case to begin with. If you plan

137

on proceeding, the onus is on you to establish irrefutable guilt, such that will convince even the skeptic."

"Are you suggesting I begin with a tainted jury?" asked Marcus.

Ishiguru, unwilling to get into an argument of semantics, and also knowing he was on shaky ground logically, raised his voice in exasperation.

"You will begin accepting jury members or I will do it for you!"

"So, if they say there is no way in hell they could ever find the defendant guilty, am I still obliged to accept them?" chided Marcus.

Ishiguru ignored the question. "Send in a whole new group," he commanded of the bailiff, then dismissed even those jurors present, but not yet questioned, attempting to *reset* the process.

Laughton gave a cursory examination of woman number twenty-five, avoiding any direct reference to religion whatsoever—only nearing the matter by asking if she considered herself a moral person, banking on both the probability of her theism and Marcus' refusal to relent.

"And where do your morals come from?" asked Marcus. Ishiguru immediately cut off the juror and warned the counselor of nearing contempt for the court—a charge which Marcus would willingly face had he not feared his case being thrown out altogether, the judge citing Marcus' antics as an excuse for untriability.

In a tired drone, Marcus readdressed the potential juror with as benign yet fundamental a question as he could phrase. "Is there any reason you should not be able to objectively weigh the evidence and, if need be, find the defendant guilty?"

The woman hesitated. "Oh," she said, stalling. "I never really thought it out that far." She put her forefinger to her chin in contemplation. "I'm not sure if I could find him guilty," she confessed.

Marcus turned to the judge and threw up his hands in exasperation. Ishiguru cradled his head in his arms, still clutching his gavel, which waved high above him like a flag of surrender.

The judge considered dismissing the entire jury pool and calling another group, withholding from them the name of the defendant, but he knew that in itself would be substantial grounds for mistrial. At the end of the first day, two hundred of the two hundred fifty people were interviewed, and only one was deemed non-biased. The percentages were working in Laughton's favor.

In the interim days, Laughton filed for Batson to be extended to cover strikes based on religious affiliation. The issuing of new jury duty summons was delayed until after the appellate court could hear the new motion. Marcus argued in court that religion is a signifier of philosophic choice, a freely opted stance, and thus his objections were not without merit, as they were not contrary to happenstance, such as race or gender, but mindset, which is directly relevant to the issue of objectivity. Laughton argued that Marcus wasn't targeting against one religion, but targeting for one group—atheists, which was tantamount to only allowing Jews to sit jury for a Muslim or vice versa, under the guise of neutrality. Marcus rebutted, noting he never asked the religion of the jurors but rather their potential for objectivity, the bare requisite as an impartial peer. In the end, though the court was not willing to extend Batson to exclude questions on religion, they found Laughton's argument sound and decided against Marcus' blockade of all but one belief—in essence deciding nothing, as the ruling also acknowledged the prosecutor's right to question the juror's objectivity. The impotent decision threw jury selection back onto Ishiguro's lap. He opted to use the juror questionnaire as a primary factor for dismissal and had them sent out en masse to prospective jurors' homes prior to them being pooled. Only those who claimed to have objectivity were ordered in.

Seven months later and three new mailings of hundreds of jury notifications, Marcus finally allowed for twelve people and four alternates. To say the jurors were agnostic would be ambitious. At best, they were lapsed theists, dashed with one or two atheists and, if Laughton was right, at least two who had lied about their beliefs specifically to exonerate God. In short, the jury was not the prosecution's ideal.

Chapter Six

Marcus moved the jury to tears with heart-wrenching stories of accidental death, murder, suicide, rape-murder, genocide, and the like. Following each testimony, Laughton asked if the witness saw God interfere with the operations of man. None claimed to have personally seen God's mechanism; though, one Bosnian woman said, "God was there, but he was silent." Laughton went so far as to call a rebuttal witness—the serial killer James Calvish—who testified the killings were all his idea and not God's. Marcus toyed with the notion of rebutting with a killer who claimed he operated under God's orders, but the prosecutor instead chose caution, as those who claimed divine interference quite often gave questionable testimony.

After a week of witness statements depicting heart-wrenching atrocities, the defense finally acquiesced and acknowledged *bad things happened to good people*. Judge Ishiguru agreed the prosecution had firmly established the magnitude of bad things to good people, and no more testimony would be needed to establish said position.

Once having determined that man was victimized, Marcus needed to define the link between the atrocities and God's reckless actions.

However, he couldn't simply wait to see if God would testify in his own defense, and get God to incriminate himself. Circumstances had to compel the defense to put their witness on the stand. Marcus believed there are two main reasons a defense does not put its client on the stand. Either they are afraid their client's testimony will reveal guilt elsewhere, or the accused is so inarticulate he will come across as guilty. Otherwise, juries really want to hear defendants state their nonculpability. Since Marcus did not think God would come across as inarticulate—though possibly smug—he reasoned the only point in withholding his testimony would be because he *might* intentionally acknowledge his acts. God may not even recognize the legitimacy of the courts, believing himself to be above the mechanisms of man's law. Fortunately for Marcus, Laughton definitely wasn't above man's law, and he could be sanctioned, so he had to present his best defense. And, if he felt putting his client on the stand was the best response, he would do so. In this light, Marcus thought it prudent to plan on forcing Laughton's hand instead of God's. Laughton would respond in the best interests of his defense. Plus, putting God on the stand would only add grandeur to the already epic standing of this legal case. Laughton would likely use any provocation as an excuse to create a more sensational and memorable trial.

Still, Marcus had to establish the link between God's actions and the victim's plight convincingly enough to compel the defense to have their client testify, challenging the credibility of that central accusation. Only then could Marcus cross-examine the accused, which would likely result in the revealing of other grounds for attack or general obfuscation. The latter response could be either good or bad. It would be bad if, in the confusion, the jury couldn't retain its focus on the charge; good if the jury became annoyed by the apparent dodging of questions by the defendant.

The drama of week three of the trial was akin to the motion argument regarding free will. Laughton cunningly referenced Ishiguru's decision on the motion to establish the court's acknowledgement of free will, hence its right to hold man responsible for his actions. Since the demonstration of divine responsibility explicit in predestination was closed to Marcus, he rebutted by establishing with expert theological testimony that will, once granted, was often interfered with by divine intervention.

"Take the story of Job for example," testified Professor Hutchinson of Florida State Theological Seminary, and author of *The Bible Contradicts* and *Faith without Fantasy*. Hutchinson and several other key figures had been assembled by Marcus' assistant, Maria. At first, the prosecution was going to present Howard Schiller, noted séance buster, general skeptic, and author of *Born to Belief* and *Where's the Sense of That?* but the prosecution team decided a member of the theological community would be more damning and less reactionary.

Hutchinson continued. "Job was tested to see if his faith would stand divine interference. His free actions were tainted by the misfortunes cast upon him. Perhaps his faith would be different had he been allowed to be complacent. Perhaps Satan erred in taking away instead of giving to Job, creating reasons to be vain and unappreciative. Either way, I find a Calvinistic understanding of predestination confusing in light of the Job account. Why test Job or anyone if God already knows the course of our decisions. But that's the conflict, isn't it? Being omniscient, he should know all our future choices, Right? Of course, there is an alternative. Maybe God does know, and it is only Satan and the others who are unaware God knows all. Funny that man would be sure of God's omniscience but Satan, who hung with him, wasn't privy to that bit. But if that's the case, God's just having a little fun, playing with a stacked deck, pretending there is free will just to make bets with Satan who isn't the wiser that the fix is in."

"Objection, Your Honor," interrupted Laughton. "We've already established the fix is not in, and man is responsible for his own actions. I move to strike all the good professor said regarding free will."

"Your Honor," Marcus interjected, "are you prepared to make a ruling on the moral of the *Book of Job*, right here and now, in addition to implicitly declaring which religious sect has the correct interpretation?"

Ishiguru hesitated. He pursed his lips and mulled over his words. "I am not making any decrees about anything in the Bible. But, for the purposes of court, we are going to assume free will and the potency of law, got that?"

"Yes, Your Honor," cowered Marcus.

"Professor Hutchinson, please limit your testimony to God's interference as it pertains to a freely capable man."

Hutchinson smirked, relishing watching others flounder in the ambiguous waters he often treads. He spoke conversationally, his legs crossed, thin grey hair combed over, and striped shirt clashing with his patterned slacks—all a humorous combination of attributes for a man casually insinuating the culpability of the Creator. "Well, God acts as if man *was* given free will from the start. Adam and Eve were expelled from the garden for an act contrary to God's orders. Eating the fruit was an act of free will, even if Adam was coerced. One can't be lured if he can't choose."

"And of course, there's Jesus. Isn't his presence a ripple in the pure stream of free will? When Jesus cures the infirm, don't options open up to them; and perhaps others close? What about those he didn't cure and the resentment that causes? Will the thief steal in his presence? It's not what one does in church that is of significance. It is what people do when they forget about God. In truth, if you want pure free action, you would have to remove the knowledge of God's omniscience. People would have to be unaware God is watching and judging for men to behave on their own volition. If they are behaving only because they are under review, who is to know what they would do unobserved?"

Marcus let the rhetorical question hang unanswered and peered at the jury. The olio of citizens and their stoic faces betrayed little about their future decision.

Laughton remained seated and relied on his baritone voice to command attention. "Is it your contention that my client can interfere *by watching*?"

"By watching the results of the arena he constructed. It's like saying a little boy only *watches* an ant through a glass he holds for the magnification of the sun's rays."

"Then, shall I assume you believe we should hold city officials responsible for every death due to criminal activity because they did not somehow figure out a way to protect every individual, thus creating an arena of malevolence?"

Marcus rose. "Objection, Your Honor. The witness is not an expert on government."

"No, Your Honor. He is an expert on judging omnipotence," mocked Laughton.

"Enough," reproached Ishiguru, and directed his next comment to Laughton. "Please keep your questions to theology and not civil legislation."

Laughton rose and circled slowly his table, building the tension for the jury. Then he sprang, walking directly toward the witness. "What atrocities are you claiming are documentarily attributed to God?"

"Well, the Bible cites . . ."

"I'm sorry, who wrote the Bible, before we cite it as proof?" interrupted Laughton.

"It's the word of God," said Hutchinson.

"It is? Approach, Your Honor."

Marcus joined Laughton at the judge's bench.

"Your Honor, Mr. Hutchinson is using a document as his source yet to be validated as authentic. How are we to know it really describes my client's words and deeds?"

"We can ask him if he wrote it or dictated it," offered Marcus.

"But, counselor, he's not on the stand, and he is not going to incriminate himself if he does take it. You're gonna have to provide the writers so I can challenge their credibility."

"Your Honor? It's the Bible," gasped Marcus.

"Sorry Marcus," replied Ishiguru. "Until you can demonstrate we are hearing true accounts of the defendant's actions, you or your witness cannot reference that book as recorded fact." He shooed the lawyers away. "Professor Hutchinson, I'm ordering you not to use the Bible as historical record. Please confine your answers to your personal knowledge."

Hutchinson lost his grin and looked to Marcus, confused.

Laughton continued. "What consequences are you personally aware of God creating?"

"All. None. It's hard to say."

Laughton paced a loop, sizing up the jury, who looked back in expectation. He abruptly turned to Hutchinson and fired off his question. "Are you aware you are accusing God of committing acts of depraved indifference?"

Marcus gasped at Laughton's blunt question. He never expected him to lay it all on the line like a gambler pushing his chip pile onto one number at the roulette wheel.

Nor had Hutchinson expected the bluntness of such an accusatory ploy. He preferred to partake in a didactic discussion on theology, not to be reminded of having his words implemented into judicial action. He stammered and looked to Marcus. Laughton used the hesitation as a theatrical cue. He raised his arms out about his sides, and stood in anatomical position, as if to ask *what gives?*

Ishiguru did not wait for the objection. "Please answer the question."

"I … I suppose I never thought about it," replied Hutchinson, shifting in his seat, a man fallen from earlier certitude.

"Well, you are aware I am an attorney for the defendant, and he," gesturing toward Marcus, "is the prosecutor; and you are his witness?" he mocked.

"Objection, asked and answered," hoped Marcus, watching Hutchinson's testimony self-destruct.

"Asked, but not answered," replied Laughton.

"Yes, he said he never thought about it."

"Take a moment now. What do you think?" Laughton weaseled a question under the objection.

"My objection, Your Honor?" reminded Marcus.

But Ishiguru waved off Marcus with two upward flicks of the wrist without unsettling his cheek from the palm of his other hand. Ishiguru was interested in the answer.

Hutchinson responded almost apologetically. "Well, I certainly don't mean to insinuate God doesn't care."

"You are testifying on behalf of punishing God for his acts."

Marcus shot to his feet once again. "Objection, the witness has testified to God's influence. He is not an expert on the legal repercussions of such actions."

"He is also insinuating my client's intent, which is exactly what is in question," responded Laughton.

Marcus immediately rebutted. "God can have a chance to clarify his intent after I establish his actions."

"True …" pondered Ishiguru. "Your client can defend his actions. Let's move on from this line of questioning and hone your scope to one of action's relevance."

Laughton smirked and turned to the weary Hutchinson. "Has God ever acted in such a way as to make you think he should be found guilty of depraved indifference?"

Sweat trickled down Hutchinson's brow as he peered over to the complacent defendant. Marcus saved the professor from having to answer with another objection. "Your Honor, that is clearly just a way of back-dooring the punishment question in lieu of asking the professor about his true area of expertise—God's actions."

Laughton responded. "Surely the professor's students have asked him the *whys*. Doesn't he ever delve into God's intent at the university?"

"He doesn't have to *speculate*," enunciated Marcus. "God is here himself to explain his reasons."

"But, Your Honor," replied Laughton, "the witness is not obligated to testify. I'm not sure he will, and that shouldn't remove our right to challenge motive."

Marcus broke protocol and directly addressed the witness during the prosecution's examination. "Do you know what goes on in God's mind?"

Hutchinson, startled, became defensive. "What? No."

"Your Honor?" singingly pleaded Laugthon.

Marcus continued. "My point, Your Honor, is the defense is the only one demanding this witness address intent. Motive is an issue Mr. Laughton is pushing to assuage culpability. The prosecution needn't speculate here on the defendant's justifications if it doesn't wish to wade in potentially ambiguous waters."

"Firstly, please refrain from addressing the witness until redirect," reproached the judge. Marcus nodded. "So, you have no motive?" inquired Ishiguru.

"We have means, opportunity, and action. It suffices to say his motive could purely be satiating his own megalomaniacal whims."

"Come on, Your Honor, now who is testifying as to intent?" whined Laughton. This time, Ishiguru employed his hand gesture to hush Laugthon.

The judge raised his cheek from his palm. He shifted in his seat and looked toward the ceiling as if the answer were above him. "I don't like it," he began. "He is your expert witness. And his scope is not merely one of action, but of all theology to include the mysteries of motive. I've changed my mind. I am giving Mr. Laughton latitude."

Marcus' shoulders deflated, and Laughton released a grand huff as if his own execution had been stayed. "Thank you, Your Honor," said Laughton. He turned to Hutchinson, who was now near panic. "If you believe my client interfered—and, mind you, we disagree on that front as well—what do you think his reasons were?"

"I ... I wouldn't know," fretted Hutchinson.

"Could the reasons then be justifiable; perhaps some *if not for my client, all mayhem would ensue*-type of justification?"

"Sure. Again, he is omniscient. I don't mean to suggest he doesn't have good reasons." Hutchinson looked pleadingly at God. "I'm sorry. I am not judging you. I've devoted my life to your word."

God remained stoic. Laughton sat. "No more questions," he said, waving away the witness.

Marcus remained seated, ruing not having called Schiller as his subject matter expert. Schiller wouldn't have wavered. Yes, he would have turned off some of the jury with his certainty, but now Hutchinson's vacillation was creating the same division in the jury.

"Are you through with the witness," Ishiguru asked Marcus.

Marcus resigned himself to standing in the hopes he could kick start a rebuttal, though he was unsure where to begin. "Just one or two more questions, Your Honor." He didn't check to see if the judge acknowledged him.

"So, does it sound like the prosecution is saying to you, 'His client didn't do it, but if he did, he had a good reason for it'?"

"Objection," retorted Laughton, feigning being insulted.

"Counselor," said Ishiguru, warning Marcus.

Marcus nodded and commenced pacing while talking. "Regardless of God's reasons, good or bad in intent, is it true that God influences man merely due to his presence?" Marcus asked hamming up the question with a flourishing bravado.

"Well yes, that's fair to say," replied a somewhat relieved Hutchinson.

Marcus continued. "And is it also fair to say *influence* is in opposition to free will?"

"Well ... it *could* be a factor in freely choosing," hedged Hutchinson, nearly backtracking.

"A factor that must be considered? Which is different than choosing without the awareness of a creator?"

"Who's to know?" replied Hutchinson.

"Suppose there is a tribe isolated from the rest of the world that never believed in a deity."

"There aren't any."

"But for argument's sake suppose there is one," continued Marcus. "Could they possibly behave differently once they are told of God?"

"They could."

"And if we are told one thing is evil and another is good could that influence our decision as to which course of action to take?"

"It could."

"Sounds like God *is* an influence to me. Thank you."

Laughton called from his seat. "Redirect, Your Honor." Marcus was getting tired of Laughton's back-and-forth rebutting, as if whoever ended with the witness would win. It was the legal version of *getting in the last word.*

Laughton began with his customary head of steam. "When the prosecution gave you that fabricated scenario of a tribe without a deity concept …"

Marcus stood. "Objection. The defense's verbiage is caustic," he said, attempting to break Laughton's rhythm.

"It *was* fabricated. Your own witness testified there is no documented evidence of a tribe without a deity concept," responded Laughton.

Ishiguru, as if he were ignoring two meaningless complaints by children arguing over who got more milk, merely told Laughton to continue.

"As I was saying, when the prosecution *created* the scenario about a tribe without the deity concept, why is it you said there weren't, or aren't any, or such?"

"Because every known society has a religious belief system."

Marcus stood. "Objection, speculative. Does an atheist's society have a religious belief system?"

Laughton responded. "Sure, they think it is bunk."

"You know darn well you are saying every group believes in at least a single if not multiple deities."

Ishiguru pondered the objection and then addressed Hutchinson. "Is an atheistic group even deemed a society?"

"Not by the strict definition of the term as used by anthropologists."

"Could you define the term for us, please?"

Hutchinson happily recited a scholarly definition spiked with his own casualness. "A society is a long-standing group of people bound by a cultural ethos, common language, dress, behavior, and such, often within a geographic proximity; as opposed to some group that merely meets from time to time to discuss an idea."

"Thank you," said the judge. "You may continue," he directed Laughton.

"Why do you suppose every society has a god-concept?"

"I suspect it is because the god-concept has an explanatory value that helps instill cohesion and ethical behavior, even in societies otherwise appearing immoral, like say the Inca with their proclivity for sacrifice. It is still better than the uncertainty of a chaotic system."

"So, would it be fair to say the god-concept keeps order?"

"Yes."

"Is it responsible for any other good effects?"

"Of course. There are a plethora of religious groups doing things like feeding the poor or aiding the infirm here and abroad. And that's just the tip of the iceberg."

Laughton shrugged to the jury as if to say, "Need I say anything more?"

Marcus stood as soon as Laughton turned to make his way back to his seat. "Do you mean like the good order of the Crusades? The order of the Taliban? Or the order of the Bosnian wars?"

"In my view, there would be greater chaos and more division in those areas if there weren't any stabilizing belief system. Though reprehensible acts occurred, it's nothing in the face of havoc."

"Isn't it true the god-concept has, in itself, created havoc?"

"What's the alternative? Anarchy? That by definition is havoc."

Marcus addressed the judge. "I am done with this witness. I would like to call on a surprise rebuttal witness."

"Your Honor," knee-jerked Laughton, thinking up a particular objection, "the … the prosecution is rebutting its own witness. They can't open their own door for rebuttal."

Marcus ignored Laughton's logic. "He will give testimony directly refuting the defense's position regarding the necessity of a god-concept, which opposing counsel opened up; not me."

"I was intentionally baited," griped Laughton.

"And you bit," responded Ishiguru, and turned to Marcus. "But I warn you, counselor, your witness is to keep his testimony to the importance of a god-concept in assuring for order, or morality, or the like. He is not to testify on any other matter."

Marcus agreed and called on Professor Corey Maze of the Massachusetts Institute of Technology: another find by Maria. Professor Maze strode up to the witness box. He wore khakis, an open dress shirt with jacket, but no tie, and what Marcus remembered to be Wallabies without socks. His curly black locks, in addition to his hip manner and dress, made evident to most faculty and students why he was nominated annually for *Teacher of the Year*. Maze was the kind of teacher the students called by first name, the kind who could debate Popper over pizza or talk hockey at a society event.

Maze smiled warmly and Marcus, barely registering the greeting, carefully began his questioning. "You heard the previous witness say the god-concept is important because it gives a society a cohesive moral ground in opposition to the immorality of anarchy."

"It can."

"Is it the only concept that can instill morality? Can there be a moral foundation in the atheist's world?"

"Perhaps more so," replied Maze, placing his overlapping hands upon the top knee of his crossed legs.

"Can you please explain?"

"My academic specialty is game theory. I made a proposal to a bunch of programmers to come up with the most stable system, one that would assure the greatest chance of survival as revealed by an iterated game of *prisoner's dilemma*."

"Please explain the game."

Maze addressed the jury, realizing they were his main pupils. "*Prisoner's dilemma* is a game in which two criminals, isolated from each other, are separately interrogated and offered the same plea agreement. Each is facing one year in jail, but if either turns on the other, the stool pigeon will be let free while the other gets five years. However, if both testify against each other, each will be sentenced to three years in jail. The dilemma is to come up with a strategy that is in your best interest. If you turn on your companion, maybe he'll also have turned on you, and you both do three years. If you trust him, maybe he will still turn on you, and you will do all the time while he goes free. Obviously, the wisest option is for both to clam up and each do one year. But, in an itinerated game of *prisoner's dilemma*, players learn what the other previously chose and then get to choose again in round two, three, and so on. They can *get even*, or try to *win over* the other, or follow whatever philosophy they desire. We designate points for the prison values, and the program with the least amount of prison time wins. We can compare this to, say, gathering food. Hoarding food will have its immediate benefits but gain no friends to help get through lean times. Giving all your food away is self-destructive. Sharing is equivalent to both prisoners keeping their mouths shut. In game parlance, we call those that give, *doves* and those that take, *hawks*."

"And what did you conclude from your itinerated tournament?" asked Marcus.

"In the end, the doves were dominated by one mutant hawk. And the hawks always turned on each other. The most stable system was one based on reciprocal altruism. For example, a bird acting as a dove, altruistically picking the nits off its neighbor, will remember the latter and be more hawkish in the future if the neighbor doesn't reciprocate that act and instead flies away. In that sense, the bird will not waste its time when it could be looking for food or building a nest instead of having to find another bird and start from scratch with a new grooming partner. In my game scenario, the first bird was labeled a dove if it continued to waste its time picking nits off unreciprocating hawks. He would eventually die along with his altruistic-locked genes. Yet, the hawk, when faced with a group that remembers his selfish-monopoly will not find any bird to aid him once the doves die out. That is why the most stable system is one base on initial reciprocal altruism with a memory for past actions and a response system appropriate to the action. In my tournament of the itinerated *prisoner's dilemma*, a program called *i4ni* won. It began altruistically then simply mimicked what the other did in the past. It played all the other programs, itself, and two controls: one of only hawks and one of only doves. *i4ni* scored the lowest, winning the experiment."

"Does that mean every sensible dove has a little hawk in him?"

"Sort of. One must temper his reactions with a fuzzy criterion of intolerance. If a bird wastes your time, you don't have to kill it, wasting energy and potentially ostracizing yourself. You can just censure or ignore it. If it attacks your eggs, that's another story."

"So atheists can be moral under this system?"

"Sure. Without it, they can be just as immoral as everyone else. Atheism is no moral precept. Atheism is merely a cleaning of the slate. An atheist decides he does not appreciate the capricious nature of religions' moral guidelines; and he chooses to abandon them, starting afresh, lest the unsubstantiated philosophies muddle his behavior. But, he fails in his efforts if he stops there. He still needs to find a moral framework if he is looking for the survival of himself in particular and mankind in general."

"And you suggest embracing reciprocal altruism with a fuzzy tolerance system?"

"Absolutely."

"But can't one live a life of despotism? After all, there are rulers who lived to a ripe old age being hawkish bastards, right?" prodded Marcus, addressing the counterargument prior to Laughton's cross, in an effort to take the wind out of his adversary's sails.

"Sure," continued Maze. "And there are doves who survived without opposition—though, usually on the backs of others who physically defended their freedoms. But these are the exceptions. Our genes could hardly bet their reproductive survival on the rarity of being a successful tyrant, as opposed to a dead bully—the victim of a collective backlash. It would be equally absurd to create a survival philosophy of *don't get hit by a meteor* in reaction to the rare anomaly."

Maze continued. "But in answer to your question, *yes*, there will be the few exceptions to the moral precept. However, when one considers societal pressures, it is ridiculous, in fact hubristic, to believe one can insure against all events. The best a dictum can do is advise, not guarantee. My point being: it is just as impractical to behave like Mahatma Gandhi and offer the other cheek when Hitler is exterminating your friends and family, as it is to be the Nazis taking by force. In the end, even if it takes longer than the regime of one particular tsar, bey, despot, or even dynasty, the system that succeeds is one that assumes friendship, but will not tolerate abuse and ultimately will apply force to repel life-and-limb threatening force. In the end, reciprocal altruism with a fuzzy tolerance base thrives … more often than any other system."

"So, are you suggesting we should build a moral system based on evolutionary theory?" asked Marcus.

"I'm suggesting our moral system *is* based on evolutionary theory, our pangs of injustice, our sense of guilt. If we were parasites, elephant seals, praying mantises, or even chimpanzees, our morals would be different, but we're not. We're social primates with few non-microbial extra-species competition, distinguishing ourselves from other species by an ability to construct a complex notional reality—perhaps driven by a sexual arms race and enhanced by language acquisition—allowing us elaborate planning, a byproduct of which is our ability to consider other's reactions—ultimately gaining us the ability of empathy. Our sense of moral conduct is hardwired by selection. And any philosophy regarding moral behavior prior to or without incorporating Darwinism is downright suspect."

"It sounds like Spencerism. Wasn't that tried before, and it failed miserably?" asked Marcus, trying to cover all of Laughton's possible angles.

"His was a bastardized understanding of evolution. When the Rockefellers, Gettys, and the other barons defined the term *fit*, they did so with a misunderstanding of the times in which we evolved. On the savannah, during the Pliocene, in the millions of years we developed the tools for survival and social interaction, there was no monetary wealth. In fact, too much material possession would be impossible to protect or transport and therefore a deficit. The Inuit rightly say 'the best place to put a surplus of food is in someone else's stomach.' To associate Darwinism with monetary success is an absolute misunderstanding of *fit*. Money making has no meaning during man's longest period of existence. To make allies who would assist you in protection, resource gathering, and all the benefits of a unified community, while you pass on your genes, is everything. Ayn Rand is wrong in associating money with moral righteousness because she overlooks that wealth can be gained by ill-gotten means, freakish business fads, or simply be inertly inherited. Yes, if you make a dependable product and others pay you for it, you can more easily obtain necessities, and that does seem to jibe with evolutionary fitness, but why? By what standard is your business conduct deemed *good*? What differentiates tyranny from integrity? Ultimately, your stability is susceptible to the balancing nature of reciprocal altruism with a fuzzy tolerance system. The integrity of your acts will be siphoned through the group's evolved moral code."

"And this morality is without a god-concept?" summed up Marcus.

"Yes. Though it does resemble one of the main Judeo-Christian tenets: 'Do unto others …' Perhaps, the evolutionary authority is the reason for that tenet's universal familiarity as the *Golden Rule*. And perhaps that is why, seemingly in jest, many people also revise the rule to, 'do unto others as they do to you.' Innately, we desire to be self-protecting reciprocal altruists. That judicial desire is what ensured our existence as a species. We should embrace it."

• • •

A middle-aged housewife wearing a floral-pattern dress, sensible shoes, and carrying an oversized purse with long inflexible leather shoulder straps rose from the jury box without gaining so much as a glance by anyone else in the courtroom. While rummaging in a large bag with straps jutting straight into the air, she walked toward the edge of the book's pages and into the margin, where the page numbers appear. The woman pulled out a small yellow steno pad and returned the purse to her shoulder. The housewife peered beyond the book and read from the note pad: "And now a word from the author:"

At this point, I would like to address you, the reader. I have provided some blank space so you can jot down any concepts lingering in your head, such as: "Wow, that was the most insightful stuff I've ever read. Now, I understand everything about everything," or "What a pedantic piece of junk. Thank God, I am almost done with this book so I can move on to the upcoming bestseller, 'Da Vinci, Dante, Austen and other names to drop in a book title' or 'My pricey handbag, my Tao, and other ways to insult chicks with lit.'"

Either way, I've copyrighted these following pages along with the rest of the book. Once your thoughts are entered, they are in my domain; so, please don't use them again without my consent. (Well, it is my book). Insert amazing personal observations here:

Displaced People

The housewife standing at the margin regained the reader's attention. (That's your cue to read on. If you are not ready for this cue, ignore the afore-written sentence, continue with your thoughts, doodles, lunch, or whatever, and, when ready, begin with, "The housewife standing at the margin …," skip all the other stuff, and pick up … wait. That's all too complicated. Just pick up here):

The housewife standing at the margin regained the reader's attention and directed his or her—depending on certain anatomical additions or subtractions—gaze to a group of characters loitering around the book's binding.

"What in the hell is the big holdup?" the Corporal asked the housewife. "I'm tired and hot, crammed in here with all these people. I'm sick of these boots and cammies, and I'm sick of all this waiting. I don't get the point of any of this."

Father Atkinson shook his head, annoyed by the rudeness of the Corporal; though, he too was growing impatient. "Do you have any idea how much more of this trial scene we have to sit through?" he asked.

The housewife appreciated the reverend's courtesy. "I can't imagine there is much more. We seem to be making some headway, in the book if not the trial," she said while thumbing through her yellow note pad. "The prosecution has nearly concluded the tired cliché of reproaching God. And we got through the *cool* professor's didactic worldview narrative."

"Why are we asking her? What the hell would she know about anything?" demanded the Corporal. "She's a minor character. She doesn't even have a name." He peered down, shuffling pages with his feet. "Can anyone see how many pages are left?"

"I don't see why you are even concerned," said Tay Po. "You've already got multiple ink-space. This is the first I've appeared, and I may not even be written in again if the opposing forces don't invade Cortinia."

The Corporal snickered. "Even if Op4 does invade, your name will probably never be mentioned," he jibed.

Po looked forlorn. The idea of appearing in a novel unbeknownst to the reader had never occurred to him. Suddenly, he lit up with a bright idea and blurted out, "I'm five-five with black hair, thin frame, and brownish-olive skin. Damn, that's too common. I know; I'll walk with a limp. I'll rip my shirtsleeves off. Remember what I look like! Remember me! Remember me!"

"Dork," sneered the Corporal.

Specialist Moody leaned into the Corporal and whispered in his ear. "Shouldn't we detain the guerilla?" he asked, motioning to Po with his M16.

"Are you that fucking stupid?" responded the Corporal. "We're in limbo—nowhereville. Nothing here matters. Go shoot him if you want. Hell, shoot yourself while you're at it."

"Why would I shoot myself? I've already made my appearance in the story. I wouldn't be written back in. There is no more use for me."

"Then what are you doing here?" asked the Corporal.

"Bored."

"Why don't you frisk her," the Corporal said pointing at the housewife. "Maybe she's smuggling a bomb in that fucking monster of a handbag."

Half from embarrassment due to the Corporal's expletives and half from his own impatience, Father Atkinson suggested the woman return to the trial scene in hopes of getting the novel back on track. Unfortunately for him, the Corporal took up his cause. "Yeh, get the hell out of here. What's the point of all this crap anyway? Like the reader is interested in what us characters do when we aren't on. This whole novel sucks ass if you ask me."

Father Atkinson began to physically shoo the juror. "Go. Go. They're waiting for you, I'm sure."

The housewife left the margin while the specialist tried to corral Po, who, in turn, grabbed the guard's rifle butt and attempted to wrestle it from the soldier. Unamused, the Corporal nonchalantly threw letters from words already read by *you*, in an attempt to knock this page number out of the book.

The woman crossed the white gap and entered the black text of the novel right here: The middle-aged housewife returned to the jury box and took her seat without being noticed by anyone in court.

Marcus had finished his examination of Maze, and Laughton came out of the gate with his customary head of steam. "Mr. Maze, you say we should act in accordance with our evolutionary instincts, that our innate morality will direct us. But isn't it true our morality is not a product of Darwin but of *God?* If not, we would all think it appropriate to go around raping nubile sixteen-year-olds—or do we?" he mocked.

Maze coolly responded. "No. Though we may desire to have inter-course with them. But, we must weigh the impact of our actions. If being lecherous to a near child gets us ostracized, losing our allies, we would not be acting in our best interests. Now, there are those who do act—influenced by immediate gratification—and they may gain a temporary support network, but they chance the larger group of reciprocal altruists objecting and taking away their freedom, incarcerating them or worse. Clearly, the repercussions are not in the best interest of the lech.

"In the same vein, one can gorge on chocolate due to our evolved desire for sweets, but a healthily functioning human, considers the repercussions of obesity. The sensible being's ability to consider long term ramifications—an evolutionarily selected trait—outweighs the immediate sensation.

"Conversely, we can also use contraception and violate our gene's main point of survival—reproduction. But, again, our reasons for such action are complicatedly tied up in the evolutionary ancestry. There were no artificial contraceptives during the majority of our existence as a species—just as there were no chocolate bars, internet porn, or table manners. Evolution is without foresight. It did not superficially prepare for future cultural ethics—the customs and courtesies of our present environment—but it does affect the core principles—the fundamental moral structure. Though it did not prepare us to frown upon those ordering a second dessert, it did instill the desire for our allies to be healthy. It did not prepare us to keep our elbows off the table, though it did instill a sense of agreement, however silly or misguided, as long as the courtesy is not detrimental to existence. It did not instill in us a notion pornographic images will not get pregnant, though it did make us want to be desired too.

"Ultimately, evolution shapes our ethics as siphoned through cultural influences. Genes are merely potentials, needing a specific environment to be actuated. The fundamental moral system is in us, ready to work. For millions of years, there existed killing, rape, and conversely cooperation. And, yes, there were repercussions to attempting to physically impose one's will on another. Does that answer your question?"

"Um-hm," said Laughton instinctively taking pause, knowing he was playing in the wrong league. Maze intimidated him; and when intimidated, Laughton became what he thought of as *cute*.

"Getting back to your computer game with the prisoners, are we to assume man evolved with the threat of prison-time over his head?"

"Are you seriously asking me that?" replied Maze.

"My point being, you created the criteria of the tournament, right?"

"Yes."

"And you are the one who decided survival is rewarded with points?" continued Laughton at a distance from the witness box, building up slowly as if he were gingerly walking on rice paper.

"That's based upon the fundamentals of evolution," Maze responded.

"Isn't it a little presumptuous of you and your *game*," said Laughton, trivializing the word, "to assume self-interest is the purpose of morality? Couldn't morality be equally likely to wipe us out, due to our dovishness, yet still be a higher ideal, one rewarded in an afterlife?"

Maze immediately responded. "There is no evidence for an afterlife, so I can't speak to that. But as for defining morality in a fashion that sacrifices you, your children, family members, and loved ones to the most horrendous of circumstances—such as starvation, rape, pains of torture, and ultimate death—well, I wonder at your alternative definition."

Laughton considered continuing, but he worried that his extended pauses unnerved the jury as they did himself. "That's all," he muttered and meekly returned to his seat, realizing he couldn't end his defense on that note. The strength of Maze's testimony would be damaging as the last resounding voice prior to summations. Laughton knew what he had to do.

Chapter Seven

"Please state your name for the record."

"God."

The bailiff looked to the judge to see if the brevity of the name would suffice. Ishiguru nodded.

"Aren't you going to swear me in?" asked God.

"We don't do that anymore," responded Ishiguru.

"Thank goodness. It served no purpose anyway. And I hated being associated with all those liars who took the stand and gained credibility just by invoking my name."

Laughton began his customary pacing of the jury box—a dramatic display of thinking, like a drum roll leading to his question. Then, he dove right in.

"Who is to blame for the wrongs in the world?"

"Man."

"But didn't you create man?"

"Yes."

"Then aren't you ultimately responsible?"

"Is each parent ultimately responsible for every wrong deed done by his child?"

"No. Not in this courtroom, they aren't," Laughton said, more to the jury than to the witness.

"Exactly."

Laughton continued. "You heard the prosecution's witness testify your presence in itself interferes with free will."

"I allowed for that."

"Why is your presence necessary at all?"

"If I let humans run amok, they would eventually lose the notion of good. They must be exposed to divine purity so they can recognize it as a viable option."

"So, you are not steering them one way or the other?"

"On the contrary, to steer them would be to tarnish the outcome."

"Why don't you interfere and save those who are suffering or about to suffer?"

"Say there is a man about to commit a horrendous act upon another individual. For me to interfere would mean I take away any chance of the individual changing his course of action and ultimately finding grace. It would be the equivalent of sentencing a man prior to his committing the crime."

Laughton played devil's advocate. "What if he were a repeat offender?"

"Again, even in your courts, you're wary of over emphasizing past acts when trying a particular action and sullying the judgment. The individual's past may still be judged, but his past should not be assumed as his future."

Laughton performed another of his crucifix-like gestures—arms extended, palms out, implying a self-evident truth, as he returned to his seat.

Marcus stood.

"So, you are innocent because you gave man free will. Is that your defense?"

"Yes."

"And you created free will?"

"Yes."

"And you created everything?"

"Yes."

"And you are omniscient?"

"What was that? I wasn't listening?"

"I said, and you are …"

"I'm joking. Yes, I'm omniscient."

"Then, if you are all-knowing, shouldn't you have been able to foresee what each person would do with his free will?"

Laughton shot to his feet. "Objection, argumentative. My client should not be held responsible for man's actions after giving them free will. Either a thing is a bull or a cow; it's not both."

Marcus retorted. "I am asking if he foresaw the end result of the granting of free will."

"I'll allow it," Ishiguru ruled.

"Yes, I do know how each person would respond with free will. I know all," said God.

"Then why shouldn't you be held responsible for the actions resulting from the granting of free will?" demanded Marcus.

"Because I did not commit those actions."

"Didn't you indirectly commit those actions since you began the process ultimately resulting in those acts?"

Laughton bounded up once again. "Objection, now the prosecutor is in direct opposition to Your Honor's previous ruling against determinism. In motions, you ruled man's acts are not fated."

Ishiguru pondered the objection while rolling his cheek across his open palm. "Objection sustained. Counselor, please refrain from assuming man is impotent of will."

Marcus thought how to reapproach any question insinuating determinism. "If you are omniscient, then what is the purpose of testing us?"

"Who in the blazes says I'm testing you or any man?"

"What about Adam, Job, Abraham, and the others?"

"The story of Adam is bullshit. Job, Abraham … bullshit. Do you believe everything you read?"

Marcus didn't expect this.

God continued. "Come on. It's evident the Bible was written by man. It contradicts itself. I had more influence on Einstein's papers. I created you. I know you inside and out. I don't need to test you to know what you are made of."

"Then why all the suffering?"

"Why all the beauty? Why anything?" God responded.

Marcus waited as if there would be an explanation. After a moment, he realized his question had been reduced to an abstraction.

"You still haven't answered my question. If you created everything and you know everything, then why shouldn't you be held responsible for the bad as well as the good?"

"Man commits the bad."

"But being omniscient, you should have seen it coming. Couldn't you have avoided it? Wasn't there something you could have left out or added to make us better?"

"Like what?" God smirked at the stupefied lawyer.

"Well, how would I know? I don't claim to be omniscient."

"So, you are trying me for not doing something: that which you have no idea what?" asked God.

"Neither I nor any man has any idea how you do what you do, but that doesn't detract us from asking why you do it."

"It should," replied God.

Marcus foresaw this problem with cross, but he tried to power through, nonetheless. "Are you going to answer my question?"

"About something I could have done to ease human suffering?"

"That's right," persisted Marcus.

"Yes, I could have rid man of a brain. No nervous system, no pain."

Laughton let out a loud guffaw, and the courtroom filled with titters. Marcus realized his fishing expedition was coming up dry. He decided to return to the personal approach so successful with the testimonies earlier in the trial.

"Do you know a David and Judy Flieshman?"

God shifted in his seat. For the first time since the trial, he appeared mildly apprehensive.

"I do, of course," God affirmed.

"And where are they now?"

Laughton sprang to his feet once again. "Objection. Where is the counselor going with this? It has already been acknowledged bad things happen to good people."

"Subject to connection," responded Marcus.

"Get there soon," warned Ishiguru. "I will not be going backwards in this trial."

"Where are they now?" continued Marcus.

"Not on this temporal plane."

"That's where they aren't, but my question is where *are* they now?"

God hesitated. Marcus quickly approached, feeling footing for the first time since this cross. "Permission to treat the witness as hostile, Your Honor."

"It's your funeral," Ishiguru reflexively said before he realized the purport.

Several courtroom spectators blurted out, "Amen." Marcus shot a sideways glance at the judge, who tried to cover his awkwardness with a cunning smirk.

"Didn't they die in a car accident?" continued Marcus.

"That's true, provided we overlook the semantics of the word *accident*," responded God.

Marcus reflected for a moment, avoiding God's bait to get back into a debate on determinism.

"Isn't it also true they were both devout Jews, mitzvahed in their respective temples?"

"Your Honor," said God, addressing Ishiguru. "Isn't the level of spirituality a private matter between the Fleishmans and their confessor?" he asked, pointing to his own chest.

Ishiguru nodded. "Yes. I suppose their religious conversations are protected communiqué."

Ara 13

God turned back to Marcus and smirked.

"Can I at least ask if they were Jewish?" inquired Marcus of the judge.

"Not of him."

"Well, would it surprise you to find out they were mitzvahed?" continued Marcus.

"No," acquiesced God.

"Supposing they were Jews, which according to Temple Shalom and their daughter, Jackie Maiser, they were; where would they be, now they are dead?"

"I already answered that when I said they were no longer on this temporal plane."

"Are they in heaven or hell?!" shouted an exasperated Marcus.

"Right now, they are in Denver," replied God.

"What? No. Not their bodies. You know what I mean. Where are their souls?"

Laughton sprang to his feet and emphasized his "Objection" by pounding his fist on the tabletop. "Your Honor, the existence of souls assumes facts not in evidence."

"How about it counselor?" asked Ishiguru.

"Well, don't we have souls?" Marcus meekly asked, realizing his assumption.

"What are you calling a soul?" God playfully replied.

"I don't know … I suppose a being—a self—beyond the material self."

"What is it made of?"

"I don't know." Marcus' hands flailed about as he looked for the right words. "Whatever is left of man after he dies, to the exclusion of his body."

"The memory of them is left," offered God. "A meme, perhaps."

"That's material—synapses and such."

"But, it is not of their body, as you insisted. It's of someone else's."

"Then what is left to the exclusion of everyone else's material *too*?"

God's face lit up. "Oh that thingy. That's in Boise."

"What?"

"What?" responded God.

"We can't be talking about the same thing," replied Marcus, confused.

"Possibly not," agreed God. "It's hard to follow your train of thought."

"What were you calling a *thingy*?"

"Objection, Your Honor," sang Laughton. "Your instructions said the line of questioning would be allowed as long as it was subject to connection. So far, there has been none. He's clearly fishing."

"The witness is pretending not to understand my questions," complained Marcus.

Laughton continued his objection. "The prosecution is asking about a *soul*—something outside the scope of material. As such, Your Honor, I move it be found immaterial."

"Really counselor," Ishiguru warned Marcus, "the courts are no place for irrelevance. Please keep it material."

"What about the notional?" asked Marcus.

"Fine," agreed Ishiguru. "We can all acknowledge there is a notional concept called *soul* existing in our minds in the material form of synapses and nerve impulses or such. Now, move on from there."

"May I approach, Your Honor?"

Ishiguru reluctantly beckoned the counselor over to the bench. Laughton let out a loud sigh as he labored to his feet and moseyed over beside opposing counsel.

Marcus waited for Laughton. "Judge, a good deal of my case rests on the notion the defendant justifies his behavior with the promise of bliss in an afterlife."

"It was never our position such a promise was made," interjected Laughton.

"It's acknowledged doctrine," said Marcus.

"That's hearsay," responded Laughton.

The judge beckoned Marcus closer to the bench and leaned forward, over his crossed arms, compressing his chest so he couldn't speak above a mutter if he wished. "Counselor, you haven't, in my mind, sufficiently established that the defendant had a hand in any malfeasance to begin with, let alone his justification for such crimes."

"If I can establish the reason, the act will become clear."

Laughton didn't hesitate, relying on his proclivity for idioms. "That's cart-before-the-horse logic, Your Honor. It's akin to claiming a motive for murder prior to the acknowledgment anybody's missing. Earlier, the prosecution lacked motive and complained the intent would be revealed if the defendant took the stand. Well, we obliged, and now they can't establish a crime, so they are seining for reasons one would be committed. Is there anything concrete?"

"He's right," agreed the judge. "This fishing has to stop."

"Why don't you pursue that megalomaniacal motive and ask him why we should revere someone who has created the stars, Earth, man, and all other living things?" mocked Laughton.

"Enough," responded Ishiguru, waving the lawyers away. It mildly disturbed him to agree so often with such a bona fide jackass as Laughton.

Marcus paced around the witness box, gathering his thoughts. He was beginning to doubt God was culpable in any wrongdoing. "You were pursued, were you not, for your alleged crimes?"

"I was," affirmed God.

"And you fled?"

"I really never went anywhere beyond the scope of a hexahedron, the entirety of which is no bigger than a breadbox."

"A book," guessed Marcus.

"A book. Now, each individual copy in which I appear may have traveled; and the owner may have been fleeing—more likely on a cruise to the Cayman Islands—" God's aside was aimed at the judge who smirked in reply; "but I myself never fled in material space."

"But you went to Auschwitz, New York, and Cortinia?" said Marcus, puzzled.

"Only in the book."

"OK, OK. So you fled notionally."

Laughton expressed his objection from his chair. "Again, immaterial, Your Honor."

Marcus turned to Laughton. "I don't think you are using the term correctly." He faced Ishiguru. "The point being, the defendant's impulse was to flee. How he fled is irrelevant."

"I'm not sure you have established that his impulse was to flee," said Ishiguru.

"Then I request some latitude, as it goes to the defendant's state of mind."

Ishiguru nodded and Marcus returned his attention to the witness. "When you were in Cortinia …" Marcus caught himself, "in Cortinia in the book, didn't you create havoc?"

"It wasn't havoc for me."

"But it was a state of havoc for others."

"I suppose."

"In fact, didn't you outright highjack the book from its author and derail the plot from its intended course?"

"How does one highjack a book from the guy who wrote it?" asked God.

"Haven't others accused you of such?"

"Objection, hearsay," called Laughton.

"It's the defendant's direct knowledge. I am not asking if it is true, just if he was directly accused of it," explained Marcus.

"I'll allow it," said the judge.

"Well?"

"I suppose others thought I was trying to make a hodgepodge of things so the book would never see light of publication."

Marcus continued the reasoning. "The less sense the story made, the less likely an agent or publisher would find it credible?"

"That's the logic."

"In fact, you renamed the book from *Displaced People* to *Drawers & Booths*, a nonsense title, merely because the author has trouble pronouncing those words, making it even harder for him to promote."

"I like the new title. It's catchy."

"Ultimately, the author would realize the futility and scrap the whole project altogether?"

"Is the counselor testifying?" interjected Laughton.

Marcus ignored the half-objection, and Ishiguru, too, glossed over it. "What would happen to your pursuer if that were the case?"

"I suppose he would never catch me," said God.

"Because it would fail to be written?"

"Objection, Your Honor," interjected Laughton. "This is all supposition and *what ifs*. Is there any evidence my client caused the havoc in Cortinia?"

"Well, how 'bout it, counselor?" responded Ishiguru.

"I can connect later by calling a witness who will present such testimony."

"Who?" asked Laughton.

"We will inform the defense once we know we can procure such person."

"I have a right to know who," demanded Laughton. "Besides, it's much too late in the trial for the prosecution to add a witness."

"Your client opened the door to rebuttal," replied Marcus, relying on the explanation's earlier success. "I will make my source known once we have him as a witness."

"Then you currently have no witness to confirm such allegations?" inquired Ishiguru.

"No, Your Honor," admitted Marcus.

"Well, until I approve said person, please refrain from mentioning him; and I also caution you from further speculating as to the defendant's behavior in Cortinia until there is corroborative testimony."

Marcus sucked in his cheek and stared at God, wondering what he should ask next. After all, it wasn't every day he could have a candid discussion with the Creator—if one could call it candid. A question came to mind, but he dared not ask it in this arena. If only he were the defense, he could have all the private conversations with God he wanted.

Laughton likely didn't make use of the time. He was probably too afraid of his client's scrutiny.

"No further questions," Marcus said and fumbled to his seat as if through a fog—dejected and alone.

Chapter Eight

Marcus, Maria, and Lewin, Esq. sat around the large oval conference table, brainstorming and thumbing through numerous pages of testimony, law texts and even the occasional philosophical tract.

"I don't see the problem with claiming we have a rebuttal witness," said Maria. "We can subpoena Hattie Shore, and he'll testify that God created havoc in Cortinia."

Marcus replied in a slow dirge-like speech. "How would he know? The most he could state is havoc occurred, but he has no real knowledge how. It's not as if he saw God pulling strings like a puppet master. The lines of cause are assumed. We can't present his assumptions as a rebuttal. I've been down that road over and over again; and it's a dead end."

Lewin, Esq. let out a sigh. He decided to recap the essentials, hoping to kick-start an idea. "We need to establish God was directly responsible for the havoc, which in turn will give credence to his desire to flee, insinuating his acknowledged culpability. From there, we would establish that his flight was fueled by guilt for his participation in man's suffering. That's a lot of assumed connections. And we are still for want of the initial proverbial nail. It's impossible to have firsthand knowledge that

God directly caused the havoc of Cortinia," he concluded, feeling more hopeless than before his summarization.

"Maybe there *is* someone," replied Marcus, nearly disappointed.

"You've had someone in mind all along, haven't you?" asked Maria. Marcus shrugged. "I don't understand," she continued. "Other than God and Hattie, who else has direct knowledge?"

"There is one other," said Marcus.

Chapter Nine

Marcus stood and looked over the press pool—familiar faces that daily congregated in the court since the trial's start. He scanned the pews, taking cursory notice of the other spectators, an olio of grieving, revering, or just plain curious onlookers—those less aggressive than the demonstrators thronged outside the courthouse, picketing and shouting "Give God his Freedom!"

The attorney turned to the jury and gave a half-hearted smile, still unable to steel himself for his next move. Laughton noisily stacking the edge of papers encouraged Marcus to find his voice. The counsel for the defense had already been apprised of the next witness—the rebuttal witness—that is if Marcus could control the testimony enough for it to have any rebutting value. The prosecutor turned to the judge and announced the name of the third person who had any knowledge of events in Cortinia and who could appear outside the story's confines. "I call to the stand Ara 13."

The audience and press, none of whom were privy to the name added to the witness list, broke into a chorus of awed wonderment. The jury, collectively stunned, held its breath. Only Laughton and God appeared unrattled. Laughton continued to noisily move his papers into various stacks, and God sat with an expression of jovial certitude.

The courtroom guards opened the far doors, and Ara entered in theatrical fashion. He wore sneakers, blue jeans and a black T-shirt onto which he had bleached the words "I Wrote This Shit." Ara strode right up to the witness box, entered, sat, and leaned forward, eager. Marcus rounded his table and approached the witness. The prosecutor's apprehensions returned as he remembered the absurdity of Witness Prep.

Earlier, Marcus had contacted Ara by phone, asking him if he had any knowledge about God's actions in Cortinia. Ara said he had *full knowledge*. Marcus swallowed hard then asked Ara if God created the havoc in Cortinia. Ara said *yes*, but he wasn't working alone. "How do you know?" asked Marcus.

"Because I also created the havoc in Cortinia."

"I don't understand," replied Marcus.

"I will see you in a few moments," said Ara.

"But I called Galveston, Texas and I'm in New York City. It will take you several hours. We'll set up a flight and transportation from the airport ..."

Marcus was startled by a knock on the window of his office door. He cautiously got up and scrutinized the figure smirking back at him. Marcus slowly opened the door and craned his head around, keeping his body behind the glass barrier. "Yes?"

"It's me, Ara."

Marcus had only a cursory remembrance of the actual *prep*. Mostly, he recalled Ara sitting smugly and avoiding inquiries with a simple, "I got that all covered."

"But, I really need to know what you are going to say," replied Marcus. "I can't keep shooting in the dark. I don't want any surprises."

"Look. I'll be frank with you," confided Ara. "It's going to all be surprises for you."

"Why does it have to be that way?"

Ara continued in his understanding manner. "It just makes for better drama. My stuff would lose its impact if I were to reveal here what I can drop like a mega-bomb in the courtroom."

"You can tell me now, and it will still have its drama in court for the jury, judge, and spectators. I, myself, don't appreciate the drama."

"I know. That's what makes it funny," said Ara.

Marcus didn't remember much else from the discussion other than his own resurfacing desire to ask what he wanted to ask of God. But again, he just couldn't get the question out. Unfortunately, it, too, was the kind of question that would make for good drama inside a courtroom."

After meeting the fledgling author, Marcus' day shot by in a flash. He didn't remember going to sleep, eating breakfast, lunch, or dinner, driving, using the bathroom, talking with his colleagues, or anything else likely to have happened prior to his arrival in the courtroom today.

Staring downward, Marcus mindfully paced the area in front of the witness box as if he were diligently creating a crop circle with his footwork. He was thinking. He couldn't remember the questions he had readied for the witness. Hell, he didn't even remember preparing any questions, which, of course, would be ludicrous.

"Just start talking," said Ara. "The right words will come out."

Marcus looked thoughtfully at the confident witness. He was afraid to speak. But he was also afraid to continue futilely matting down the marble floor.

Ara's soothing words spoke only to him. "Just begin."

"Were you in Cortinia?" asked Marcus.

"I was," Ara replied.

"Did you see the havoc that occurred there?"

"Oh, wait. I thought you meant *for real*," said Ara. "The havoc that occurred, only happened in the Cortinia of my book. I was actually at a training center in Louisiana which is also dubbed Cortinia. But, that one was real. The Cortinia in the book is a notional place based upon my real-life experiences. The type of havoc you are referring to, the one of a literary nature, did not occur in reality. I invented it as a metafictional device."

"It all seems so confusing," remarked Marcus.

"Only to characters inside the book. It is perfectly evident to the reader. Some think the device is cute, some think it is trite, but no one has difficulty understanding the boundaries."

Marcus probed further. "And it's not evident for those in Cortinia?"

"Oh shit," laughed Ara. "I'm sorry. When I mentioned those inside my book, I wasn't just referring to the characters in Cortinia. I was talking about you all too."

"Who all?" Marcus asked, addled.

"You, Marcus. The judge, jury, spectators, press, opposing counsel, peers—everyone," Ara said, gesturing to the room in entirety.

The courtroom burst into a cacophony of groans, objections, and general complaints of disbelief.

"Surely, not everyone!" piped up God over the din of the crowd.

Marcus turned, taking in God's comment and rotated back to the witness. "We can't all be characters in your novel?" asked the lawyer.

"For good or bad, that's what you are," Ara replied.

"Well, it would help if you offered some silly silly form of proof."

"Excuse me," interjected Ishiguro, "but did you say *some silly silly form of proof?*"

Marcus stopped, thrown by the interruption. "I most certainly did not, silly."

"Did you just call me *silly?*" asked the judge. A few titters escaped from some jury members, and the giggles were passed on to the press pool. Marcus stood aghast. Ishiguro pounded his gavel in an attempt to gain order. He found the jeering to be a direct affront to his professionalism. He raised his voice above the titters and demanded, "Silly, silly sill silly sill!"

The court erupted into guffaws and Marcus turned about, taking in all the laughing people.

A huge swan flew over the witness stand, swooped down upon Laughton's neatly piled notes, grabbed a stack with its beak, and made a mess of the remaining documents under the current of its fluttering wings. Laughton shot back in his chair, scraping across the beach sand, and clutching the chest of his Hawaiian shirt in frightened contempt. The giant green lobsters in the jury box laughed and mocked the counselor through the use of their antennae with gestures obscene in the lobster kingdom.

Insulted, Laughton stood and reproached, "Silly, silly, silly, sill, silly silly;" then dropped his plump chin to his chest, certain of the cogency of his criticism.

Marcus faced the witness box, ignored the crabs sidling by, and exclaimed to Ara, "Silly, silly, sill, silly, anymore, I believe you! Please make it stop!" When he finished, all reverted to the originally written scene.

Holding back tears of fright, Marcus asked Ara, "Am I really just a character in a novel?"

"Yes," said Ara, simply.

Shocked by the inauthenticity of his reality, Marcus asked the question haunting him since the trial began. "Am I gay?"

"Objection, relevance?" But the judge, still in shock, ignored Laughton.

Ara smiled at Marcus, paternally. "No, you are not gay."

"I'm not?"

"No, that's what makes your predicaments funny."

"They are not funny to me," replied Marcus.

"None of us is finding humor in any of this," said Ishiguru. "I have too large a workload to have my time wasted on someone's rankly amateurish literary hopes."

Jerry McClurry stood from among the press pool. "Don't you get it, you jackass? You have no workload! You don't exist outside of this freakin' trial!"

"Who the hell are you?" asked Laughton.

"Nobody," said Jerry. "I figured if we are all characters in a book, there really aren't any repercussions for me speaking up and getting my own ink."

Marcus turned to Ara. "Can you cut that out? It's so distracting. I can only imagine the confusion you caused the reader by inserting such peripheral characters into the scene."

Ara nodded his agreement and Jerry disappeared—to the horror of the Associated Press reporter seated next to him, who convulsed into hyperventilating bouts of coughing hiccups. His photographer shook him by the arm in an attempt to silence him, but to no avail; Ara wrote the reporter out of the novel, and the hyperventilating man vanished before all. Marcus shot a reproachful look at Ara, who shrugged matter-of-factly. Among the pool of spectators, a baby began to cry. A woman gave a half-muffled shriek, stood, and with baby in tow, raced out of the courtroom.

"Why are you doing all this?" asked Marcus.

"Short-term, it makes me laugh. In the long-run, hopefully it will be deemed literarily inventive and launch my writing career."

"And this is what the people want to read about—lawyers having sexual identity crises and women with babies being scared out of their wits?"

"I'm hoping so."

Marcus paced between the judge's box and the lawyers' tables. He stopped and in surrender asked, "What now?"

"Well, I plan on continuing the trial," said Ara.

"Don't you think it's getting too didactic?" blurted out Laughton, immediately regretting his interjection.

"Do you think I should break it up with some more gibberish-inspired scenes?"

"No, no," replied Laughton, sinking further into his seat.

Marcus turned to the judge. "Can we proceed with the trial?"

Ishiguro looked to the weary jury, lawyers, and audience before inquiring of Ara, "It's been a long day. We could all use a break to gain our wits. How about we adjourn until tomorrow? Would that be OK with you?"

"Sure, I'll make a chapter break and see you all *tomorrow*," Ara replied.

Chapter Ten

"Is that better?" asked Ara.

At first, the judge didn't understand Ara's question. It seemed like no time had elapsed since the last chapter. But then it occurred to him he was feeling generally refreshed as if newly showered. He observed that the lawyers were wearing clothing different from their attire of the previous chapter. They too noticed the change in clothes and the feeling of invigoration. One of the jurors went so far as to acknowledge a knick on his face from shaving that wasn't there pages ago. In fact, unlike yesterday, it was raining.

"Feeling better?" asked Ara.

"Yes, much," replied Ishiguru. "Thank you." The judge swiveled to address the counselors. "Are you all feeling like new and ready to proceed?"

"Yes, Your Honor," they said in concert.

"Very well. Where were we?"

"Marcus was exploring the idea that I was ultimately responsible for the happenings in the Cortinia of the novel," replied Ara.

"Oh yes, please continue," said Ishiguru, motioning toward Marcus.

"In your book, did God create the havoc of Cortinia?"

"Hmm, that's the distinction, isn't it?" began Ara. "Yes and no. But, is trying God on the basis of the havoc in this book the same as trying God for real?"

"Is it?" asked Marcus.

"Again, yes and no. For me it helps. For some readers it may or may not be useful. But let's not lose sight of this book's purpose—to entertain. After all, it is fiction. Yes, there can be a moral, but I really don't want this story to be mired down in theology. I am more concerned with the character dynamics and the writing process. I enjoy having characters like the Corporal behave one way in the story and another when it is interrupted, as if he were an actor whose body of work we like but personal conduct we deplore. I enjoy having minor characters abruptly demand attention. I like having you all talk with the author and behave as haphazard devil's advocates, challenging my own personal belief system—an exercise everyone should undertake, at least in spirit. I hope to create an enjoyable read that encourages others to *think outside the box*, shake some trees—not merely for dissident value, but with the mind of a skeptic, ready to embrace the accepted belief system, but only after holding it up to the light at all different angles. I want to evoke thinking for the fun of it."

"And we are your avenue?" asked Marcus.

"Yes."

"To include God?"

"Yes."

God shot to his feet. "That's a lie!"

Marcus remained calm. "Wasn't that his own outburst?"

"No. I wrote that," Ara said.

"Can we do a little experiment to prove it?" Marcus proposed.

"Sure, like what?"

Marcus thought. "Can you make God say he is a little tea cup."

God said, "I'm a little tea cup."

A rime of awe permeated the courtroom and was inhaled by the spectators. *Wallaby*, thought Marcus, as a look of knowing serenity crept across his face.

"May I ask you your own personal beliefs about God?" asked Marcus.

"I'm an atheist."

"And what does that mean to you?"

"I believe there are two different ways of looking at atheism. One form states there are no gods. The other states one does not believe in gods. I find the first to be unscientific and borderline pompous because declaring with unquestionable certainty any theory and removing it from the realm of challenge is contrary to the scientific method. To say there are no gods is just as presumptuous as to say matter cannot be created nor destroyed, end of story. The belief may be valid, but it monumentally remains under scientific scrutiny. No theory is Babe Ruth. Their numbers never get retired.

"One can have serious doubts and rely on physical data and probability to support or disprove a theory. And our experiences may suggest that a thing's probability is infinitesimal. But experiences change. Theories never have the final word. That's why scientists don't write gospels.

"To avoid a biblical assertion, I declare absolute disbelief in gods, not absolute authority regarding their existence. To state with such affirmation there are no gods closes the mind to the possibility there is one. It is wiser to say one does not believe in gods because currently the data does not support such a concept. Like U.S. constitutionalists, scientists know laws are not written by omniscient penners. Even those concepts we find sacrosanct are subject to modification. Just ask those in prison or the military about *freedom*, or those taking a life in self-defense about *killing*.

"I, too, allow for modification and make the distinction between my imperfect beliefs versus demanding an irrefutable position. My position is refutable. It just hasn't been refuted yet. Show me rabbit fossils in the Cambrian strata or Dead Sea scroll references to DNA. Of course, if I do have a vision or witness a miracle, I will likely ascribe it to some non-divine origin, like a tumor or a currently unknown natural phenomenon. And there is the chance, if my mind fails, one can never prove to me the contradictions of my logic and the certitude of a divinity. But the difficulties caused by mental context are not the fault of the skeptics. The onus of proof remains on those making the assertion if they desire corroboration. They must establish to others my mind is awry, but unfortunately to do so, the best means is through verifiable evidence— a proof system, presupposing the universality of sensory ability. Once a thing can be verified through sensory proofs, it can be deemed *sensible*.

"For those who challenge my atheistic definition on the grounds of its refutability and equate that with agnosticism, I rebut: I have never come across any data leading me to believe there is godly or any supreme intervention; therefore, I do not currently believe in any. I am not agnostic. I have no doubts. Right now, I do not have an ounce of belief in a god. I am a-theistic.

"But, as to there actually being one—how would I know? I barely understand the question. Theist's gods have morphed from an accessible, pagan-like, Old Testament anthropomorphic personality subject to sensory proofs, into a hybrid, outside the scope of disproof, outside the framework of *this* reality. A god that is the ethereal summation of infinity, an all-being, all-present god, a god in all things, of all things has no meaning. We already have an everything. To claim a god is that everything as well, does not further the definition of everything. Remove him from the equation and we still have an everything. Gods only have identity if they can contrast with an everything. They exist only if given parameters, specificity— distinguishing themselves through speech and action—and thus, separating themselves from the everything. Polytheism presupposed this distinction, as the gods in those systems have separate identities. However, any arbitrary god-parameter is subject to whimsical debate, since there are no real criteria for verification. I believe this to be the intent. How is one to refute a position not taken? If theists avoid defining their gods, the disproof is elusive.

"This same subjectivity taints the value of cherry picking for morals from the Bible or any other book. Who is to say what parts are valid beyond finding worth in an allegorical assessment? Without the evolutionary foundation of reciprocal altruism with a fuzzy tolerance system, how does one condemn egregious acts using theistic texts and defend the notion of arbitrariness? If this process is not arbitrary, what axiomatic fountain are we tapping into when denying moral worth of particular biblical passages?

"To argue inside any theistic construct is likely a futile effort, and perhaps unnecessary. Ayn Rand is right in declaring existence axiomatic. We must acknowledge existence as revealed by our senses to construct proofs. And if we have faulty senses, reality still reacts with our defective detectors producing the net result. We can academically challenge the credence of reality—claim we are in a dream state and will wake instead of dying—but in the end, we likely come down from our scholastic theorizing and eat and not play in traffic. We assume reality in order to function in this existence; that is what sensible means, after all—as verified by the senses. Hence to act contrary to a common acknowledgement or common sense is nonsense.

"Sure, there are those who take a *leap of faith*, assume another level or type of existence, and act on that belief—perhaps destroying themselves in the process, proving their sincerity. And yes, they can claim they have proof, ignoring my earlier comments about assuming an abnormality in sensory collecting or a hidden variable. But, even if their belief is the majority, they are incapable of offering such conclusions to the scrutiny of verification. And without any verifiable data, I am forced to react only to their net result. If the manifestations of their beliefs are people being slaughtered, scientific and medical progress being stalled, intellectual honesty being corrupted, and sex being repainted as sullying, then I must question the byproduct of such a belief, not only on the grounds of intellectual verifiability, but from positive net result. Hence, theism fails on grounds of common sense and moral principle." Thus, Ara concluded.

"Then, if you don't believe in gods, why are you publicly putting *Him* on trial instead of internalizing your debate? Isn't that kind of smug?" Marcus asked.

"I suppose so. But that's the chance I take in the hope of contributing an intelligent product. Every competent attempt stems from an egotistical belief in one's own potential; doesn't it?"

"No further questions," said Marcus.

Laughton stood and apprehensively crept his way to the witness box.

"So, are you saying atheism is the cure-all for our moral ills?"

"Not at all. It is just as likely for there to be immoral atheists as morally upright theists. A lack of belief in a god does not assure moral behavior. I look upon atheism as a cleaning of the slate, erasing all moral assumptions and behavioral dictates not supported by reality. Atheism only shakes up that *Etch A Sketch* of our moral system and posits, *OK, now what.* We are still responsible for the morals we fill in the empty space. I recommend reciprocal altruism with a fuzzy tolerance system. Hence, the work is two-fold: ridding oneself of moral assumptions and obfuscations, and replacing them with a wise, substantiated system."

Laughton proceeded. "So, I just want to be certain; are you stating with absolute assurance, as the orchestrator of all that occurred inside this, well, novel of yours, my client, your literary God, is not ultimately responsible for the havoc that occurred in this said novel's Cortinia—that in reality, it was you who's ultimately responsible?"

"That is correct," Ara said.

"Am I also to assume we can carry the same logic to all the horrific occurrences inside these pages: the murders, suicides, and such were all ultimately orchestrated by you, the author?"

"That is correct."

"Thank you for your candor," concluded Laughton.

"Redirect, Your Honor," said Marcus. "What about outside this book? Say we had this trial in real life? Surely, you are not the author of reality as well?"

"No, I am not. Most of reality seems beyond my control."

"Then is not God ultimately responsible, and isn't that the purpose of this trial—to hold him liable?"

187

The author hesitated, reluctantly preparing to be the bearer of bad news.

"No. I'm sorry, Marcus. That's where you have it wrong. In reality, I do not hold God ultimately responsible for the ills of the world."

"Then who?"

"I hold man responsible. Man is the depraved, indifferent individual. But, he is also the one responsible for many of the beauties of the world: the arts, humanities, literature, music, comedy, satire, philosophy, and drama. No, Marcus, those horrors not attributed to natural disasters, are the responsibility of us. The flipside of denying gods is taking responsibility for the *evils* and ultimately doing something about them."

"What about, as you said, natural disasters, accidents, cancers, bad luck, and such? Isn't God responsible for them?"

"Not that I know of," replied Ara.

Marcus reflected. "Can I ask you a personal question?"

"Sure."

"Why are you, an atheist, ultimately coming to the aid of God in this trial? Why is it you created me, a nice guy, and Laughton, a heel; and you put me on the losing side?"

Ishiguru looks to Laughton. "Any objection?"

"What's the point?" Laughton muttered. Ishiguru nodded his assent.

"I'm sorry, Marcus, but man must take the blame for this one. I couldn't honestly write a story honoring man's denunciation of responsibility. I'm opposed to what I like to call the *Charles Barkley excuse*. Barkley claimed he was just an athlete and not a role-model, and fans excused his declaration; some even extolled it as honesty. But I respond: *You bet your ass you should behave as a role-model, but not because you are a famous athlete and have legions of admirers, but because you are an adult. And as an adult, you have a responsibility to behave honorably. That is our social contract. That is what makes our communal efforts workable. Grow up and behave, and be a good role-model to kids and all.*"

"For you to win, Marcus, would be to give credence to Barkley's excuse—to honor an abdication of accountability. In short, acknowledging reality means embracing mankind's evolved moral system, and taking the blame off any god. It means accepting responsibility for behavior. It means you lose."

Marcus stood deflated of fight. Laughton cleared his throat, and, with the assistance of the table, slowly rose to his feet. "Your Honor, at this point, I would like to move for a mistrial on account of the prosecution not establishing its case."

"Your Honor," replied Marcus, "we are well beyond a motion for summary dismissal, as the prosecution rested long ago."

Laughton pounced, knowing momentum was on his side. "The prosecution's case was revisited when the prosecution announced a rebuttal witness. Also of note, Your Honor, I did not move for a mistrial at the initial rest. I hope that indicates some validity in my current motion."

"I'm inclined to agree with you," stated Ishiguru. "Is there anything else I should consider?" he asked of the author.

"Not as of this writing," said Ara.

"Well, I don't suppose I could behave in any fashion contrary to your intention anyway," reasoned the judge. "The court of New York finds the evidence insufficient to hold the defendant any longer. God, you are a free man. Ladies and gentlemen of the jury, just because you didn't get an opportunity to render a verdict does not mean your presence was any less valuable. I thank you for your time."

The jury let out a collective sigh. Laughton shook the hand of his client while simultaneously patting him on the back.

"This doesn't excuse everything in your past, you know," said God.

Laughton gave a strangled laugh, and patted God on the shoulder one final time.

A court server walked up to Marcus during the hubbub and handed him papers. "What's this?" asked Marcus. The server walked off without replying. Marcus opened the papers and read. He was being sued by Tom and Maria for sexual harassment. He looked over to the once-defendant. God smiled. Marcus wept.

PART FOUR

Chapter One

"Corporal, wake up. Wake up," whispered the hushed burly voice, unused to restraint in volume. The tent's interior darkness contrasted with the vivid colors of his dream state, and the pitch black reality ironically shocked the Corporal's system toward waking. Franklin continued to shake the bagged mass, unaware in the darkness that the Corporal was awake.

"I'm up," said the Corporal. "What is it?"

"It's me, Franklin."

"Who?"

"Lieutenant Franklin—you know, the operations officer."

"Oh," said the Corporal, unsure as to the significance of the lieutenant personally waking him.

"There's something going on near the front gate," said Franklin.

"What is it?"

A general "shhh" permeated the cold, dark air. The Corporal expected the lieutenant to announce himself and muster the respect of rank, as many officers would have done; but Franklin was a reasonable guy who sympathized with the hard-working nurses acting as guards.

"Come outside," he said. Then whispered lower, "Don't worry so much about your uniform."

The lieutenant made his way blindly to the far flap. The Corporal expected to see a stream of light seep into the tent upon Franklin's exit, but he soon realized the hour. It was the second time he had been woken in the middle of the night here. The first was to meet the CA team. This time, he assumed things were more urgent as the lieutenant didn't send a messenger to raise him.

The Corporal reached for his boots, and, in his sweatpants—seconding as sleeping attire—he plopped his feet into his footwear and made his way in the darkness toward the end flap. His untied laces softly scratched along the floor planks as he shuffled along. Outside the tent, the lieutenant motioned for the Corporal to follow him toward an open view of the front gate.

"Nice getup," joked Franklin.

"Do I need to ..."

"Relax, Devil Dog. I'm just kidding. We aren't going anywhere. It's just you and me."

"What is it?"

Franklin stopped outside the motor pool, out of earshot of all tent occupants, but within sight of activities at the front gate.

"Starting at around midnight, there has been a small migration of individuals from outside the town toward our front gate."

"Sounds like a CA job," reminded the Corporal.

"Yeah, we went to them first. They advised the colonel not to let the villagers remain near the gate and to notify local authorities."

"And?"

"And? And nothing. That's it. The police said they can't take the squatters away because they have no place to put them; and the CA team was adamant about them not coming on the compound. But it's eerie, don't you think? I mean, should we really let these people stay there like this? And the campfire they built. S-2 is up in arms about it. I don't know what I'm thinking, but ... well, do you have any experience with anything like this?"

"No, sir."

"What about your captain?"

The Corporal now understood the reason for this visit. The lieutenant personally wanted to know what was going on. His own S-2 was tight-lipped, and the only insider he knew was the mysteriously absent PAO working with the CI teams on a supposed parade-detail.

"I haven't heard from him in nearly a week. What's today?"

"Tuesday ... well, Wednesday now."

"Yeh, wow, It's been since last Monday. You remember when he called. Otherwise, I got nothing, sir. But, if he drops me a line, I'll let you know whatever I learn." The Corporal was left mildly uncomfortable by the familiarity of the conversation. He knew the lieutenant had confided his apprehensions to him, not solely because they were both enthusiastic readers and found a common bond with rhetoric, but because the Corporal was a Marine. Also, the chain-of-command, though universal between enlisted and officers regardless of branch, seemed mitigated by the respect reservists had for full-timers.

Franklin too realized the awkward familiarity and decided to cover himself. "Of course, I don't want you to tell me anything your captain doesn't want disclosed. I was just seeing your thoughts on the matter, that's all."

The Corporal didn't want to leave the lieutenant with this clumsy half-truth and chose to reestablish his subordinate role by asking questions.

"Where did they come from?" he inquired about the squatters.

Franklin spied the area beyond the gate where a few of the villagers had set up a temporary campsite. "From the hills, I gather. The CA calls them *displaced people*."

"Are they just gonna leave them there?" inquired the Corporal.

"Kick said they needed to set up a compound for them away from us."

The Corporal observed another long, angular straggler meander up the road toward the squatters and join the group. The knobby-kneed man unburdened himself of his large makeshift pack—no more than twine and a blanket—and smoothed out an area of ground along the main fire.

"How many are there?" asked the Corporal.

"Ten to twelve, and they seem to keep coming."

The two men stood silent, watching the squatters, as if waiting for the intermittent glow of fireflies in the night, until Franklin decided to retire to bed.

"Well, sorry to have woken you. I didn't mean to spook you with this." The Corporal knew the lieutenant was telling himself he shouldn't be spooked, which meant he was.

"I'm sure we'll learn more in the morning," said the Corporal, taking his cue to retire.

"All right. Goodnight, Devil Dog."

As the Corporal returned to his tent, it occurred to him why he had been able to see the squatters on this night when only a sliver of the moon was visible, and also why he and the lieutenant felt so concealed. The high-posted lights that normally lit the compound at night had been swiveled to illuminate the outside perimeter. The entirety of the MASH unit was dark, with only a corona of light edging up to the near brush and concertina wire. This along with the brilliance of the blazing campfire finally unnerved the Corporal to the level of the lieutenant's unease. *Was the MASH unit now hiding? Was the brush suddenly a threat?* The Corporal would have to ask the lieutenant come daylight.

By morning, fifty-eight squatters had established themselves in makeshift camps outside the front gate. Security added a third guard to duty at the front gate. The CA personnel were in another area of town trying to establish a displaced persons' compound, in conjunction with the local government, ensuring the area would not seem to be a prison.

The Corporal noticed the change in behavior of the medical staff. Doctors, nurses, and supporting personnel no longer seemed to mill about jabber jawing. Instead, they now strode purposefully from one tent to the other, with the exception of several security personnel who clustered around the front gate staring at and conjecturing about the squatters.

The Corporal approached Specialist Bryant, who should be in bed now, since he was scheduled for guard duty during the night shift.

"You're up kinda late," said the Corporal.

"Yeah." Bryant shrugged.

"Any new developments?"

"Just a butt-load more of refugees, that's all."

"Did they say what's going on?" asked the Corporal.

"Our L-T is over there talking with them now. From what I gathered, they fled on their own."

"From what?"

"Don't you hear that?" said the specialist, pointing off toward the mountains. For the first time today, the Corporal realized he awoke to, and was inured to, the constant sound of gunfire.

"Is that gunfire?"

"You're a right bright Marine, aren't you?" mocked the soldier.

"Is that us?"

"Yep."

"And Op4?"

"Yep."

"How far away is it?"

"Miles."

"All those people came from the fighting?" asked the Corporal.

"Apparently so. They say there are many more on their way."

The Corporal stared in awe at the community of villagers haphazardly assembled in an arc no more than a hundred yards from the compound. He quick-stepped off to his tent, grabbed his camera and notepad—he always kept an ink-stick on him—and returned to the front gate. The security personnel saw the Marine approach with his camera and responded as if the Corporal's status had risen to one of elevated official duty. The guards parted allowing the Marine to choose his best vantage point. Though, in the past, he had no qualms about walking outside the compound, the Corporal hesitated because the S-2 officer was present. The Corporal was green to real news. Even his instincts were unsure whether or not this would be a classified event. One thing he was sure of: Intelligence wouldn't want to be around for pictures. The Corporal patiently waited nearly an hour for the S-2 lieutenant to return from dealing with the squatters; all the while, the gate guards wondered when he was going to snap into action, though they left him alone.

When the intelligence officer finally returned to the gate, the Corporal again patiently waited while the lieutenant ignored him and gave redundant orders to the gate guards.

"Don't let them in. In the unlikely event they bum-rush the gate, don't do anything brash. Send for me immediately. Of course, protect yourself and your weapons, but don't go shooting them if they just mill up to you."

The gate guards stared dumbly. After all, the lieutenant hadn't exactly told them how three people would stop more than fifty from pushing in the fence without the soldiers using deadly force.

"What if they storm us before you can respond?" asked Chavez.

"Look," said the lieutenant, growing impatient with his soldiers, "these people are docile. You saw me standing with them, and nothing happened." The lieutenant regretted bringing up the possibility of the people storming the gate. Though it was not a likelihood, he was unqualified to address it. The ambiguity of his instructions resulted from his own uncertainty on the subject.

"Just don't let them in, and don't shoot them," he ordered.

"Yes, sir," said Porter, the first to recognize the confusion of the situation. Once the intelligence officer paused long enough from instructing his men, the Corporal spoke up.

"Is there anything you don't want me to shoot or ask them?" he asked, relying on his *assume consent* technique.

"I'd really prefer if you didn't shoot or ask them anything," replied the lieutenant.

The Corporal thought about pressing the lieutenant for printable information, but he knew he would only be further rebuffed, and worse, in front of the security forces with whom he worked so hard to gain trust. The Corporal's conspicuously absent, "Yes, sir," indicated little about whether the Marine would abide by the lieutenant's wishes. *After all, the intelligence officer's wording wasn't quite an order, was it?* But still, the Corporal had misgivings about appearing to directly defy the officer's wishes in front of security, in addition to his own apprehensions about approaching the squatters.

"Sir, do you want me to do any overview shots from here," he asked, gesturing to the ground at his feet, as if to say, *I won't leave this spot,* "possibly for your own use if needed in the future? At least, we'll have them."

The intelligence officer, astutely smelling a compromise, agreed to the long-range shots.

"Just don't send the pictures out anywhere as of yet," he added.

The Corporal wondered if it was overreaching for the lieutenant to give him an order without consideration for the existing orders given to the Corporal by his own captain.

"Yes, sir," he said, glad the lieutenant let him at least look potent in front of the soldiers. After all, the S-2 officer wasn't an unreasonable guy. He was merely junior brass, taking on a great responsibility in what appeared to be an escalating situation. As always, the Corporal preferred to revere him. And again, the lieutenant appeared to be just a shade more legitimate than the rest of them, as he walked away laden with the potential predicament.

The Corporal lingered around the sere ground of the front gate, taking turns with the gate guards spitting and covering up the small pool with dry earth. Between jokes and hocks, he snapped several shots of the squatters. Then, the gate guards came up with the *brilliant* idea to capture images of spittle in mid-flight. This easily evolved into trying to capture shots of spittle in flight with a soldier positioned off to the side so it looked as if one soldier was spitting on another. Ultimately, this evolved into one soldier actually spitting on another. The Corporal couldn't help but reflect these are the people who were told not to shoot anybody.

After an hour of idle play with the gate guards, the Corporal decided to go to the TOC and check in with Franklin. By the time he departed, nearly seventy villagers had amassed at the squatters' camp. The walk to the TOC unnerved the Corporal. He was unused to all the tent flaps being closed and no people milling about. As he entered the TOC, he noticed the desk sergeant restrained his typical jovial banter. In fact, he appeared almost apprehensive, possibly even alertly taking note of who entered the tent. The guard nodded to the Marine, and the Corporal nodded back. Franklin looked up from his desk and gestured for the Corporal to take a seat at a nearby chair, vacated by the environmental officer who was *out and about*.

"Take your brain bucket off," he said. The Corporal was happy to oblige.

"What's the good word?" asked Franklin.

"There's a ton of them now."

Franklin nodded, unpleased.

"What's the CA's progress?" asked the Corporal.

"I haven't heard from them today."

The S-2 officer looked up from his papers.

"Where's your gas mask, Marine?" he inquired.

The Marine hesitantly stared at the intelligence officer, surprised by the question. Luckily, Franklin took up the pause to tactfully inform the Corporal about the change of policy. "We're carrying them everywhere now," he said.

The Corporal nodded in understanding.

"That means you too," said the intelligence officer, ensuring there was no room for equivocation.

"Yes, sir," replied the Marine, who realized the officer meant *now*. He stood and popped to his modified position of attention, said "Gentlemen," returned his helmet to his head, and exited the tent. Protocol was to carry the gas mask with them at all times, but for some reason, the Marines often slacked on this requirement. Perhaps, they didn't like to be slowed by the thump-thumping of the large case against the thigh. Perhaps, they would rather not be reminded of being in an environment where the gas mask was a necessary reality. If he thought he could get away with it, the Corporal would have told the S-2 officer he didn't bring one. In fact, his own captain wouldn't have known the truth. But, the Corporal also knew Franklin would have been helpful and issued him one from supply. There was no getting around it; he would have to strap one to his leg and suffer the awkwardness of the *damn thing*. The Corporal even pretended to soothe himself with the dictum, *better safe than sorry*.

He found the case at the exact bottom of his duffle bag. He opened the case, inspected the mask—wondered if it really would protect him from anything serious if need be—returned it to the case, and strapped it to his leg. Already he resented its bulk.

If he returned to the TOC now, the intelligence officer would know he was idle. Flaunting leisure was a sure way to get volunteered for a detail. However, with the squatters at the front gate and gunfire off in the hills, he was unnerved enough to remain inside the compound.

Reflecting on the heightened security, the Corporal thought it prudent to learn the day's passwords, though the gate guards always let him enter the MASH compound without challenge. In order to let as few people as possible see him doing nothing, the Corporal decided to inquire at the back gate about the passwords.

He rarely made an appearance at the rear post, mainly because it had been closed while the Army monumentally swept it for land mines. The Corporal passed the medics' station and strode near the inside perimeter, eyeing the thick vegetation along the way. He was startled by the suddenness of a helicopter cresting above the tree line. He jogged back toward the inner region of the compound, unsure as to where the helicopter would land.

As the copter touched down in an open stretch not far from the perimeter wire, three medics ran out of the hospital tent and made their way, heads prematurely and unnecessarily ducking the copter's blades. Along with a couple soldiers from the bird, the medics carried two stretchers, both occupied by injured American soldiers, into the hospital tent. The Corporal stared in awe, barely registering the reality of the event. He watched motionless while the stretcher bearers returned to the bird. The helicopter took off back over the tops of the trees and disappeared into the distance along with the roar of its blades.

The Corporal scanned the compound for another witness. A supply officer stood frozen nearby. He caught the Corporal's eye and shrugged off the gravity of the moment. At a distance, across the camp, Franklin and several other officers returned to the TOC. They must have just received the *heads up*, the Corporal surmised.

If he hadn't left his camera back in his tent, the Corporal would have snapped a few pictures, capturing, perhaps the first American soldiers to be injured in combat here. His instincts as a journalist finally kicked in, waking him from his daze. He jogged back to his tent, unlocked his duffle bag, and fished out his camera and notepad. He stuffed the notepad into his cargo pocket, something he rarely did, having been inculcated into not using his pockets. Stateside, it would wreck the starched, pristine nature of his uniform. Here, his uniforms were neither starched nor pristine, but the habit of not using cargo pockets remained.

Having acquiesced to attaching equipment to his body, he slung his camera over his head and shoulder and across his back, which in turn kept either hand free to hold onto the gas mask's case when its thumping began to annoy him.

He jogged to the TOC and composed himself before unzipping the flap and entering the tent. Franklin and the other officers were clustered in the colonel's office. The Corporal stood near the operations officer's desk, choosing not to presumptuously take a seat in a vacant chair without being offered one by Franklin. The environmental officer was not in the TOC, and the Corporal supposed he was with the CA team ensuring healthy conditions at the displaced persons compound under construction closer toward town.

The colonel saw the Corporal and gave a karate-chop wave, almost a salute. The Corporal popped to attention then relaxed, an alternative to waving back. The CO's acknowledgement steered the other officer's attention to the Marine, including Franklin, who came out of the office.

"Real-life stuff, huh," he said huffing his mild dismay.

The Corporal nodded. "Do you think I could get anything on it?" he asked as a journalist.

"I don't know if there is an official version yet," replied Franklin.

"Well, the official version has to come from somewhere, right?" responded the Corporal.

The lieutenant scrunched up his face, unsure if he wanted to assist the Corporal, but incapable of being unfriendly to him.

The Marine pressed on. "Could I talk with the colonel and find out what he is comfortable with printing?"

"I don't know that he is comfortable with any of it right now, to tell you the truth. I'm not telling you not to do your job, Devil Dog. It's just we are in uncharted waters here."

The colonel emerged from his office, as if on cue.

"Hello, Marine."

The Corporal popped to attention again.

"At ease, Marine. I suppose you are wondering about the possibilities of a story?" While the colonel spoke, the intelligence officer approached the CO from behind and openly eavesdropped. The colonel carefully considered his words, a demeanor reminding the Corporal of his own chief warrant officer back in the States. He supposed it was par for higher brass.

"Two soldiers where just medevaced to here. We know they're casualties from fighting with insurgents in the mountains." The Corporal felt important, being briefed by the colonel in front of the other officers and the few enlisted personnel inside the TOC. He also appreciated that the colonel was comfortable apprising the Corporal of events, prior to informing him of what he would want in print. The Colonel obviously understood the function and scope of public affairs. Even so, the CO still expressed the need for patience regarding publication, which the Corporal appreciated more than being ignored altogether.

"Now, I don't know yet what we would want to see in print. Mind you, I'm not trying to tell you not to do your job, Devil Dog. I just need to clear some things with State."

"Yes, sir. I wouldn't write or photograph anything such as this without your consent, sir," assured the Corporal.

"Good man," replied the colonel, paternally squeezing the shoulder of the Marine before returning to his office without giving any formal dismissal. The Corporal and Franklin exchanged meaningful glances. *Wait and see* was the order for the day.

"One thing's for sure;" proffered the intelligence officer, "soon, this little fleck of the world is going to be on the map. You, Corporal might be at the right place at the right time."

The S-2 phone began buzzing, and the intelligence officer jumped to the receiver. Displaying restraint, the Corporal remained out of earshot of the conversation. When the intelligence officer finished, he rejoined Franklin and the Corporal. "They opened up the back gate," he said.

"What about the mines?" asked Franklin.

"They finished sweeping for them. The 4-32nd is sending us personnel. Now that we're linked up, they have an interest in our security," he said without sarcasm.

The intelligence officer entered the colonel's office and sat waiting to provide an update once the CO finished with his phone conversation, which appeared like it would take awhile—the colonel's hands massaging his own scalp as he talked, like he was trying to ease the words going into his brain with craniosacral therapy.

"Let's check it out," said Franklin to the Corporal, referring to the rear gate.

The Marine waited while Franklin strapped on his gas mask and donned his Kevlar helmet. They exited the tent and headed to the back gate. Once they cleared the hospital tent, the gate came within view. A small convoy of vehicles was lined up at the entranceway—two inside the compound and two others waiting to enter. As he neared the gate, the Corporal recognized the Marine talking with the sergeant on guard duty. Overseeing much of the activity was his captain—Hi "Horse" Tate II. Captain Tate had been dubbed *Horse* when, in front of his entire platoon, the CO told him to "get off his high horse," unaware of the homophone with his first name. The nickname *Horse* stuck. In another life, his precision would make him perfect as a city homicide detective.

Accompanying Horse was one of the CI members—a nondescript soldier without a name-tape and eyes aware of *the big picture*. Oddly, the soldier was missing one of his chevrons. The Corporal neared, and the captain looked up from giving dictation to address his Marine as if he were picking up a conversation from an hour earlier—not as if he had been absent for months.

"Glad you're here, Corporal. There are going to be reporters soon— AP, Reuters, and the like. I want you to escort them around the two camps. You are not to go into town with them, and you should tell them the official view is they should not go there themselves. If they do, they are on their own."

"What if they ask me what is going on?" inquired the Corporal, hoping to be apprised of events.

"You are not to be giving sound-bites. The less you know, the less trouble you can accidentally get into. If they want an official sound-bite, you are to direct them to me. I will be at 4-32's TOC. Do not bring them into the TOC, but come get me. Otherwise, you are just to give them a tour of the facility. They'll get bored with that soon enough; by then, I will be able to escort them outside the box."

"Yes, sir. Sir, I'm having trouble gaining access into the 432nd."

"I'll take care of that," said the captain.

Then, without so much as an inquiry as to the Corporal's well-being, he returned his attention to liasoning between the two army units and his counter intelligence buddies.

At first, the report of the blast didn't register with the Corporal. He was still taking in the novelty of all the activity and conversation at the back gate.

As if in a dream, the Corporal saw planks of wood stream up into the air, seemingly in slow motion, at the front of the compound. Then, debris descended to earth in dramatic silence, at least to the Corporal's ears.

All at once, the onrush of sound added confusion to the already shocking scene. Soldiers barreled around the front gate like dogs in the midst of a home invasion. Yellowish smoke billowed from the woods, and the squatters scurried like mice exposed to the kitchen light. The soldiers in the convoy behind the Corporal watched in awe as the front-gate guards gathered their senses and took cover, aiming their weapons in the direction of the woods emitting the ominous, yellow smog. Suddenly, the horde of squatters penetrated the periphery of smoke, waving their hands, convulsing as they ran.

"Gas, gas, gas!" cried Horse, leading the convoy's charge from his standing position within the jeep—looking like George Washington crossing the Delaware—as the unnamed soldier drove, speeding toward the explosion. Fifty or so yards from the front gate, the captain jumped out of the halted vehicle, temporarily removed his helmet, and donned and cleared his gas mask, as did the unnamed soldier. The two men readied their weapons and raced into the chaos. The three other jeeps, two with rear-gate guards holding onto the vehicle's sides, half-in, half-out, slid in next to the captain's jeep. The troops slung their weapons and quickly donned and cleared their masks from behind the cover of the jeeps before running toward their intended positions.

The Corporal began trotting toward the front gate. Across the camp, he lost the identity of the individual soldiers. He took out his own gas mask and stopped briefly to hold his helmet between his knees while donning and clearing. He returned his Kevlar to his head and quickened his pace from the earlier trot.

Not a single gunshot was fired. The front-gate guards were so stunned by the explosion, they were initially unsure if the cause was accident or enemy. They hadn't expected to make this real-world determination. It was the captain's presence in a gas mask that confirmed the reality of the attack and reminded them of the legitimate need to put on their own protection before the cloud wafted closer.

Displaced People

As the Corporal ran toward the center of the compound, doctors and nurses emerged from the hospital tent. The Corporal couldn't help but think he was in the wrong place at the right time. He inanely resented the doctors and other soldiers emerging from their tents nearer than him to the front gate, as if they were butting a queue to a movie opening, and he had the right to admonish, "Wait your turn. I was here first."

MASH soldiers emerged from the TOC, their quarters, and other supporting units' tents. The Corporal felt unfairly last in line, though deep down, he was comforted with the idea he was safer at a distance.

As he passed the hospital, he could make out villagers running amok inside the compound. Some clutched their shirt bottoms to their faces, covering their mouths with makeshift filters. A few succumbed to the gas and writhed on the ground inside the compound. The soldiers from the convoy took up posts, remained poised, and drew a bead on each new villager running onto the compound so other soldiers could direct the villagers onto the ground and ensure no Op4 was among them. The Corporal marveled at the coordination of these trained infantry soldiers. He even appreciated their caution, as no soldier accidentally shot the panicked villagers—mainly because no one wanted the responsibility of being the first to open fire. *If Op4 had been discovered among the townspeople, the soldiers might have lost their cautious diligence.*

Several doctors broke from their role as observers, donned their own gas masks, and trotted to the front of the compound. They roped in straggling villagers who soon outnumbered the security forces confined to physically grasping one panicked villager at a time before corralling them into a group. The whole affair resembled a demonic version of *kick-the-can.*

The doctors and nurses treated those strongly exposed to the gas with water from their canteens—pouring it over the injured person's face, turned up toward the sky as if seeking divine grace.

The Corporal passed triage, nearing halfway to the front gate. The second explosion's intensity made clear the meager effort of the first attack. Though nearly knocked over by the concussion, he spun around, this time fully cognizant of his surroundings, and saw the rear-quarter fence completely disappear. The wood pulverized into fine debris. Gunfire followed as the opposing forces continued with the second phase of their effort. The Corporal suddenly panicked, realizing he was the nearest body to the true assault. The front chaos had only been a diversionary tactic, creating havoc and drawing the true infantrymen away from the genuine breach.

The Corporal took cover behind one of the hospital's generators. He pulled his 9mm from his holster, and, for the first time outside the target range, clicked off the safety with true intent.

The small band of guerillas sprinted onto the compound, led by a sinewy youth wearing generic military surplus clothing. Like some of the other men in his force, his shirt sleeves were ripped off and his pant legs were torn from maneuvering through concertina wire. The leader ran as though nursing an injury, as were several of his men. The group skirted its way down the edge of the encampment and behind the large shower facility, sweeping the air with their rifles as they ran.

The Corporal ripped off his gas mask, stuffed it down the front of his T-shirt—easier than getting it back into its case—got to his feet, and instinctively pursued the band in a small arc, using the tents as conceal-ment. He positioned himself within sight of a narrow gap between two tents filled only with the hopscotch-board-like array of ropes and spikes.

His senses heightened, the Corporal heard a soldier scurrying about inside the supply tent. A sergeant popped his head out, and the Marine held his finger to his own lips commanding silence, then gestured to his own eyes with a two-finger *v* and pointed to the gap between the tents. He motioned for the sergeant to stay low, as the supply soldier ran to a better vantage point. Before the sergeant could take up his intended position, a body appeared and disappeared in the gap of the tents, star-tling the Marine into alertness. When the following guerilla showed, the Corporal fired into the gap, hitting his target and a second who advanced into his line of fire. The sergeant hit the deck and spun around, firing in the general direction of the gap as well.

The guerillas returned fire, peppering the supply tent with rounds, as the Corporal and the sergeant retreated to the hospital generators. Meanwhile, several infantry soldiers arrived by jeeps to the front of the halted guerilla advancement and repelled the disjointed group with gunfire. Unfortunately, the Corporal and the sergeant had flanked the enemy band and were in the way of the guerilla's retreat through the initial breach. The two men cut an angle to the back gate, trying to avoid being down range of friendly fire. The sergeant pealed off to the left and took up a position inside the sandbagged barrier of the back guard-house. Nearly a hundred yards from the Corporal, the remaining guerillas scattered through the breach and into the woods. His adrenaline pumping, the Marine sprinted down the now open connector—at a safe angle from friendly fire—and scanned the deep woods for the fading movement of foliage. From within the compound, the soldiers fired spurts into the brush, intermittently, then ceased altogether. The Corporal marveled at the enemy's brazen audacity in using less than a dozen men to attack the compound. *Maybe, they didn't realize U.S. military medical personnel carry weapons. Perhaps this was a synchronized event, like a small-scale Tet offensive, and the 432nd got hit as well. Or was it a lone desperate attempt at capturing hostages?*

The Marine slowed his pace after losing sight of any movement in the woods. Due to the bends in the road, he could no longer see the gatehouse when he looked back up the connector. He wasn't sure how long he ran or how near he was to 432's compound, but he estimated he was within a mile.

"HALT! SHOW ME YOUR HANDS!" came the order from the woods. The Corporal observed a rustle in the brush fifty yards from the edge of the road.

"United States Marine!" he responded.

"SHOW ME YOUR HANDS!" repeated the soldier.

"I am a U.S. Marine! I'm armed! I'm holding my Beretta 9-mil!"

"DROP THE WEAPON NOW!"

"I'm U.S., damn it! I'm with you!"

Another soldier emerged from cover several yards from the first. "Did you see the shed in the woods?!"

"What the hell are you talking about?!" steamed the Corporal. "I was pursuing Op4! We were just attacked! They took off into the woods!"

"What about the shed?!" repeated the standing soldier.

The Corporal suddenly realized the soldier was offering the first part of the password, and he was supposed to respond with the second word.

"I don't know the damn password! I'm a U.S. Marine!" he reiterated, trying to use his anger like a passport.

The soldier hidden in the brush didn't waver in his tenacity. "THIS IS YOUR LAST WARNING! PUT YOUR WEAPON DOWN AND SHOW ME YOUR HANDS!"

The Corporal put the gun on safe and lightly tossed it to the side, ensuring the muzzle faced away from him, even though he threw the piece on the soft fauna bed. He raised his hands, elbows bent just enough to suggest an air of disdain.

"If I were you, I would be keeping an eye out for Op4!" admonished the Corporal.

"Why are your sleeves rolled like that?!" asked the standing soldier, referring to the way Marines invert their sleeves when they roll them, as opposed to the Army way of having cammie face up.

"I'm a fucking Marine! Ever hear of them?!"

"Ever hear of a password?!" retorted the standing soldier.

"WHAT'S THAT THING?!" asked the hidden soldier, still yelling all his words louder than necessary.

The Corporal was confused.

"What is that?!" asked the standing soldier, using his own weapon to point seemingly behind the Corporal.

"What are you talking about?!" he asked.

"IT'S A DEVICE!" warned the crouched soldier.

Instantly, the standing soldier dropped low. "WHAT IS THAT DEVICE?" he joined in yelling.

"DROP THE DEVICE?!" ordered the first hidden soldier.

"What device?!" said the Corporal. "I have no device!"

"NO, WAIT!" overrode the second soldier. "DON'T TOUCH THE DEVICE!"

"I still don't know …!" the Corporal looked down and spied his camera which had spun around his frame, and hung sinisterly just above his holster, lens against his body.

"That's a camera! It's not a device, it's a camera!" he responded.

"THAT'S NO CAMERA!" decided the first soldier.

"It is a camera! The lens is against my body! It spun!"

The Corporal was tiring of all this yelling. He was sure Op4 was gone by now, and he no longer felt the threat of the enemy. His adrenaline surge was subsiding, though his anger remained.

"Why would you have a camera?!" asked the first soldier, also growing tired of his full-force yells.

"What are you taking pictures of?!" added the second.

"Are you doing reconnaissance?!"

"I'M A FUCKING JOURNALIST AND A FUCKING U.S. MARINE. NOW GET YOUR HEAD OUT OF YOUR ASS, AND LET ME GET BACK TO REPORT."

The soldiers were stymied as to how to handle a man with a potential bomb who may or may not be a U.S. service member. If they asked him to remove it, he would have the advantage of getting his hands on the device. Nor did they want to approach, for fear it could be remotely detonated. They needed space between the device and themselves before they could have the person remove the item. But in the woods and on this curving trail, distance meant loss of visibility. They could have the target lie down, but then the soldiers couldn't keep him in their line of sight, as the growth would interfere with their view. They were temporarily at a standstill.

The second soldier decided they should slowly move the target up road, away from 432nd's compound, making use of trees as natural cover until they came to a straight section of road long enough for him to gain some distance, emerge from the woods, and give the man instructions to lie down with palms up, until EOD could take over.

In dribs and drabs, the soldiers maneuvered from spot to spot, ordering the target forward yards at a time. The Corporal tiredly obliged. Within sight of the MASH gate, though still far enough from the unit to avoid menacing them with a genuine threat, the soldiers found their long straightaway.

As the second sentry positioned himself on the road, an Army patrol emerged from the woods and met up with the Marine standing with his arms still raised.

"What the hell are you doing, Marine?" It was the S-2 lieutenant.

"I'm in custody of the 4-32," he responded matter-of-factly.

The S-2 soldier looked around until he found the sentry down-road. "What gives, soldier?" he asked. Seeing the others knew the Corporal, the two security soldiers relaxed and lowered their weapons. The hidden soldier emerged from his crouch, brushwood sticking out of his Kevlar helmet.

"We heard the explosions and the shooting," said the first soldier. "We didn't know if he was friend or foe. He didn't know the password."

The lieutenant looked to the Marine, who realized he could lower his hands and did so. The S-2 soldier harrumphed at the Corporal's lack of protocol. "I think we can overlook the password. From what I understand, you were instrumental in driving out the enemy."

The Corporal remained silent. He waited for the guards to bring up his device-resembling camera, but they chose not to.

"Well, Marine, you coming back with us?" asked the lieutenant.

"Yes, sir," replied the Corporal, understanding the invitation was an acknowledgement of his *soldierly* worth, all the more meaningful coming from a legitimate soldier like the S-2 lieutenant. The Corporal was even more surprised months later when he received a citation for valor initiated under the recommendation of the intelligence officer.

The MASH guards decided not to pursue the guerillas into the dense brush. Instead, they set up a strong perimeter, and the intelligence officer got on the horn with 432 and headquarters, having compiled a SALUTE report: situation, arms, location, unit, time, and equipment.

Displaced People

The 432nd provided assistance in guard duty at the MASH unit. The civil affairs team soon had the displaced persons camp operational, and their personnel quelled those near-hysteric villagers who had been gassed by providing medical care and bare necessities.

The tense two days of heightened alert were mainly enjoyable to the Corporal as his exploits were extolled again and again among officers and enlisted alike. Even the Corporal's captain participated in the praising of his Marine. Neither of the two guerillas he shot had died. After receiving medical attention, they were whisked away to the 432nd. One other insurgent was hit in the ensuing shoot-out. The medics tried to save him, but he died on the operating table.

As the days followed, representatives of the Associated Press as well as other stateside and foreign correspondents appeared, and the Corporal slid into his role as community relations personnel—the contingent duty his captain tasked him with. He showed the reporters around the MASH unit, tried and failed again to gain access to 432, and with the assistance of Kick, he brought them to the displaced persons compound. But sure enough, the Marine's captain was right; the press got antsy. They felt the liaison was more like a chaperone keeping them from gaining that prom-night prize. They wanted contact with the guerillas. The Corporal notified his captain, and Horse disappeared into town with those press still willing to follow a military escort.

Soon after the reporters had arrived, the military presence was augmented by yet more infantry and supporting units. The town hummed with jeeps and soldiers. The military was officially established at Cortinia with a genuine PC name for the mission: Operation Morale Boost.

The Corporal rode his bike into town. He no longer stood out among all the soldiers and civilian reporters, who seemed to outnumber the villagers. The mail-drop filled up again, and the peddlers returned to hawking their wares on the roads. Off in the hills, the sounds of prolonged gunfire would spark up and die down at punctuated inter-vals. The official parade, the supposed reason for Horse's presence, was scheduled for less than three weeks away. The Corporal wondered if the officials would still hold the event with the insurgents remaining in the hills. He and Franklin suspected there would be one last push to drive the guerillas off the island, or scatter them for good—or for long enough to *pretend* it was for good—thus pleasing whatever administration was in power.

That night, at 0200, the sky lit up like a night premiere at the Roxy. Spotlights cast tubular white into the misty air. The various news agencies insisted on putting their journalistic rights above the welfare of the paratroopers. With the displaced people camped inside their compound, the 82nd Airborne was less likely to have civilian interference. They preferred combat with only theoretical host nationals—those present in spirit, but not in physicality. The men and women of the MASH unit watched the deployment from afar, as if they were privy to a distant fair's Fourth-of-July fireworks display.

"It's eerie watching them come down like that," said Franklin.

"What? Under the spotlights and all?" asked Kick.

Franklin nodded, afraid to jinx the soldiers with verbal confirmation. His silence was like knocking on wood. But the green Captain Snider was oblivious to the jinx and asked, "Why aren't they shooting at them?" with the naiveté of a rookie asking a pitcher, "Hey, you know you got a no-hitter going?"

Franklin winced, though he knew his fear was merely superstitious. "They're too far off," he replied. "They're coming down well before the hills."

"Then, what's the point of them parachuting in?" continued the captain.

"It's fast; plus, they get to make an entrance for the cameras," said Kick.

"Though," said the Corporal softly, "if they landed close to the action, the press would just go there. Then the 82nd would really be compromised."

"True," said the captain, shaking his head. The other officers agreed.

Displaced People

"What will happen next?" Franklin asked the more seasoned Kick.

"They'll take over. The 82nd are some of the most competent people you'll ever meet, but they sometimes have less than the appropriate respect for nationals."

"Well, we all have the potential for good and bad," said Franklin. "Let's just hope ... let's just hope."

The Corporal considered chiming in again, but he was content to remain quiet. Somewhere between hope and fear, he set aside his beliefs and asked of a notional entity for the soldiers to have the courage to act justly—still, he feared their momentum and wondered if, in lieu of a precursor to order, all he was really witnessing were men falling from the sky.